Geronimo Stilton

THE SEARCH FOR TREASURE

THE SIXTH ADVENTURE
IN THE
KINGDOM OF FANTASY

Scholastic Inc.

Library of Congress Cataloging-in-Publication data available

ISBN 978-0-545-65604-7

Copyright © 2010 by Edizioni Piemme S.p.A., Corso Como 15, 20154 Milan, Italy.

International Rights © Atlantyca S.p.A.

English translation © 2014 by Atlantyca S.p.A.

Based on an original idea by Elisabetta Dami.

www.geronimostilton.com

Published by Scholastic Inc., 557 Broadway, New York, NY 10012. SCHOLASTIC and associated logos are trademarks and/or registered trademarks of Scholastic Inc.

Text by Geronimo Stilton
Original title *Sesto Viaggio nel Regno della Fantasia*
Cover by Danilo Barozzi and Christian Aliprandi (color)
Illustrations by Danilo Barozzi, Silvia Bigolin, Carla De Bernardi, Christian Aliprandi (color), and Piemme's Archives
Graphics by Yuko Egusa and Marta Lorini

Special thanks to Kathryn Cristaldi
Translated by Lidia Morson Tramontozzi
Interior design by Kevin Callahan / BNGO Books

14 13 12 11 10   19 20 21 22 23/0

Printed in China   38

First printing, September 2014

The Fantasy Company

Geronimo Stilton

I am a bestselling author and publisher of *The Rodent's Gazette*, the most famouse newspaper on Mouse Island. This is my sixth trip to the **KINGDOM OF FANTASY**.

Coraline

I am a fairy, and the headmistress of Coral Academy, the underwater fairy school. I am gentle but firm, and I love all of my students.

Blue Rider

I am a brave, daring, and courageous knight. I am the best of the best!

Tenderheart

I am the daughter of King Cornflower. I am a brave warrior and I have a special birthmark on my forehead. Shh! It's a secret!

Honor

I come from a long line of distinguished pens. I write the truth, the whole truth, and nothing but the truth!

Harper

I am a golden harp with an amazing voice, if I do say so myself. Some say I sing too much, but they're just jealous!

Clearfeathers

I am a small bird with golden feathers. I have a great memory and can see very clearly. I'm an exceptional guide.

TRY NOT
TO DROWN!

That morning started out just like any other.

I jumped in the shower and got dressed. Then I made myself a GOURMET breakfast. Well, okay, it wasn't anything too fancy — just a flaky **cheese croissant** and a cup of **hot cheddar**. Still, it was delicious!

Finally, I headed off to the office. As I walked, I tried to think of an idea for my next *book*. . . .

Oh, I'm sorry, I haven't introduced myself! My name is Stilton, *Geronimo Stilton*. I run *The Rodent's Gazette*, the most famous newspaper on Mouse Island.

Anyway, as I was saying, as I got in to work, I was still thinking of ideas for the *book* I wanted to write. But I was having trouble concentrating. A **RAGING** wind had kicked up outside! The wind **SLAMMED** the branches of the old tree growing right outside my office against the window panes. In the distance I could see the harbor of New Mouse City. I used my **BINOCULARS** to scan the sea shining on the horizon. The waves were **HUGE** and **FEROCIOUS**!

I shivered. Did I mention I'm afraid of wild weather?

Just then, I had another frightening thought. Today was the day of the ***Mouse Island Family Regatta***, an annual sailing competition. The winner would take home the

Family Cup. Then I remembered that *The Silver Squeaker*, my grandfather William Shortpaws's boat, would be **racing** against *The Sure Whisker*, my archenemy Sally Ratmousen's boat.

Holey cheese, I felt sorry for anyone who had to brave the **sea** that day! I was feeling lucky to be **WARM** and safe in my office when suddenly the phone rang.

Riiiiiinnnnnnnng!

I picked up the receiver and a squeaky female voice demanded, "Hey, **sailor mouse**, I need to get you a pair of rain boots. What's your PAW size?"

I blinked. "Well, I'm a size ten and a half," I answered. "But I'm not a sailor mouse, I'm a NEWSPAPER mouse. Who are —"

"How **tall** are you, sailor mouse?" she interrupted me. "I need to get you a RAINCOAT."

I scratched my head. "I'm three and a half tails tall. But who is this?" I demanded.

"Are you **allergic** to anything, sailor mouse?" the voice went on, *ignoring* my question.

By now I'd had it with this obnoxious mouse, but for some reason I found myself answering her.

"Well, I'm not really allergic to anything, but one time I —"

The voice interrupted me again. "Okay, listen, sailor mouse, we don't have all day to **squeak** it up. You've got to get on board that ship, cast off, and hope you don't **CAPSIZE**! That north wind is BLOWING strong today! But don't you worry, I've got it all under control. I'll pack everything up and get it to you faster than a speedboat at full throttle. I'll even put in our super-heavy-duty **Everything for the Water Rat** brand life preserver. On a day like today you're gonna need it!"

Now I was really confused.

"Everything for the Water Rat?" I mumbled.

"We're the best sailing supply store in all of New Mouse City!" exclaimed the voice.

I wanted to ask why a newspaper mouse would

capsize: when a boat loses stability and turns over or on its side

cast off: to untie a boat from the dock in order to leave

full throttle: full speed

life preserver: a device used to keep you afloat in the water

speedboat: any variety of engine-powered boat designed to go very fast

need ʃailing supplies, but the voice kept on squeaking.

"Anyway, beats me why you sailor mice like to go out in the middle of a **storm**, but that's none of my business, I just work here. Good luck, and ***try not to drown***!" the mouse added before hanging up.

I blinked. Huh?

Just then, my office door **BURST** open and a rodent dressed in a sailor suit rushed in. He dumped a pile of packages containing a

Huh?

Oof!

raincoat, boots, ropes, sails, oars, a life preserver, and a bunch of other stuff on my desk!

I wanted to run after him, but at that moment my phone **RANG** again. It was Grandfather William. *ACK!* He was probably calling to yell at me for not working hard enough!

"Sorry, Grandfather, *I'M BUSY*. Call you later!" I squeaked, quickly hanging up on him.

But before I could go anywhere, Freddy Fanfur, the sports reporter for *The Rodent's Gazette*, strode into my office. He ran toward me, waving the sports page in the air.

"Geronimo, this is too **DANGEROUS**!" he shrieked. "If only you had asked me earlier . . . I would have warned you!"

"Warned me about what?" I asked.

Geronimo, why?

But before I could get to the bottom of things, my aunt Sweetfur arrived, **SOBBING** hysterically into her lace hanky.

"Oh, my poor nephew! Why did you agree to do this?" she wailed.

Before I could reply, my cell phone rang again.

I stared at the number. **RATS!** It was Grandfather William again. I let it go to voice mail.

At that moment, **Daniel E. Deadfur**, owner of the local funeral parlor, arrived.

"Don't worry, Geronimo. I'll take care of your burial," he said, smiling.

"Um, well, that's nice of you," I said. Then I shook my head. What was going on around here? What burial?

A minute later my entire staff barged in. *"Mr. Stilton! Please don't go!"* they squeaked, waving their paws in the air.

Why was everyone so worried about me?

"Will someone please tell me what is going on?!" I squeaked, feeling a HEADACHE coming.

My secretary Mousella turned on the TV . . . and that's when my headache turned into a full-blown ***panic attack***!

Mr. Stilton! Please don't go!

THE SILVER SQUEAKER VS. THE SURE WHISKER!

"**BREAKING NEWS!**" squeaked the rodent announcer on the TV screen. "The bestselling author Geronimo Stilton will be participating as a skipper* in the famouse Family Cup race!"

First my eyes popped open. Then my jaw HIT the ground. Me? But I wasn't a sailor mouse. I didn't even like boats!

"Rumor has it that *The Silver Squeaker*'s crew ate **rancid** cheddar burgers last night and are unable to participate. But the owner of the *Squeaker*, William Shortpaws, said that his boat will **compete** with his grandson Geronimo Stilton at its helm!"

That's when I fainted.

I came to when a bucket of **frigid** water

* **skipper**: *the commander of a ship or boat*

hit me. Immediately, I noticed three peculiar things:

1. The water **DRIPPING** from my whiskers was salty.

2. I was wearing a sailor's YELLOW jacket.

3. The ground was moving beneath me, and my grandfather was standing over me, holding an empty bucket.

"More water, Grandson?" Grandfather William asked with a smirk.

Groaning, I stood up. "No, I'm fine," I

More water?

muttered, even though it still felt like the floor was **swaying**.

"Good," Grandfather squeaked. "Now stop wasting time, and get moving!"

I was beginning to think I was losing my **MARBLES**, when my sister, Thea, my cousin Trap, and my nephew Benjamin arrived.

"Come on, Geronimo, the **RACE** is about to begin!" they cried.

Right then it hit me. No, I wasn't going crazy. I was on *The Silver Squeaker* in New Mouse City's harbor!

Rancid rat hairs — my worst nightmare was coming true! Did I mention how much I hate boats and **CRASHING** ocean waves? With a sob, I scrambled to get off the boat, but I tripped on a line*. Then I watched in disbelief as my grandfather **JUMPED** off the boat with surprising agility, pulled up the gangplank**,

---

* **line**: *a rope or cable in sailors' terms*
** **gangplank**: *a small movable plank or light bridge used to get on and off a boat*

and untied the moorings*.

Now there was no way to escape. The ᗷoᗩt had left the pier!

"Come on, Gerry Berry, grab the helm**!" my sister scolded.

The race had begun. Thea ran to hoist the sails and I GRIPPED on to the helm for dear life.

Lightning FLASHED overhead as *The Silver Squeaker* pulled out of the harbor. I was immediately overcome by a terrible case of seasickness. Oh, how I wished I was home!

For a second, I closed my eyes and pretended I

* **moorings**: *equipment that is used to secure the boat to a fixed place*
** **helm**: *a ship's steering wheel*

was there. It didn't last long. Just then, my sister **shrieked**, *"The Sure Whisker just passed us by!"*

"We can't let them win!" Trap yelled.

Now, normally I would do anything to beat my rival Sally Ratmousen, but that day, I couldn't have cared less. The wind was growing STRONGER AND STRONGER and the waves were getting **higher and higher** and I was feeling SICKER AND SICKER.

I listened to the weather report on the radio with growing dread. This storm was one of the **worst** in over a century!

"Let's go back!" I shouted.

But no one listened.

"Don't be such a **scaredy-mouse**, Geronimo. I want to win!" Thea insisted.

"Me too!" piped up Benjamin.

"Relax, Germeister," Trap added. "I'm going to make a nice pot of tasty cheddar soup. That'll calm your **nerves**."

Right then, a huge WAVE hit *The Silver Squeaker* and sent her reeling. The sail shifted, and the boom* hit me square on the head.

Thunk!

The last thing I remember was feeling icy water covering me. For a second, everything around me went dark, and then an enormouse RAINBOW-COLORED bubble appeared before me. . . .

* **boom**: *a horizontal beam that supports the sail on a boat*

1. GREAT BARRIER REEF
2. CORAL ACADEMY
3. MYSTERIOUS SHIPWRECK
4. SEAHORSE STADIUM
5. TUNA VILLAGE
6. TORTOISE CLIFF
7. SEA GRASS GREAT PLAINS
8. SECRET LAIR OF MORAY EELS
9. ELECTRIFYING CLIFF
10. BLUE THRILL AMUSEMENT PARK
11. LOST TREASURE GROTTO
12. OCTOPUSOPOLIS
13. WHALEOPOLIS
14. SQUIDOPOLIS
15. SHARKBURG
16. ANCHOVY VILLAGE
17. SARDINE BAY
18. SEA STAR CENTER
19. DEEP BLUE GROTTO
20. FOREST OF SMOTHERING ALGAE
21. SEA ANEMONE WOODS

CORALINE'S REALM

WHY ME?

I floated inside the RAINBOW-COLORED bubble and soon found myself at the bottom of the sea, back in my regular suit. How strange! But the waters were calm, so I looked around. That's when something *TUGGED* on my jacket. I turned and came face-to-face with a puffer fish.

At first I didn't think much of it. But then the fish began to shout at the top of his little fish lungs: "Hey, you! Follow me!"

My **EYES** opened wide. Was this fish really talking to me?

"Yeah, I'm talking to you," the **FISH** said, as if reading my mind. "Follow me! Are you waiting for a written invitation?"

"Why should I follow you? I don't even know your name," I squeaked. Then I stopped.

Suddenly I became aware of three things:

1 I was **talking** to a fish. . . .

2 I had been underwater for at least **TEN** minutes, and . . .

3 I could **breathe** underwater!

The fish **ROLLED** his eyes. Then he said, "The name is **PUFFY**. Now, come on. We don't have all day."

When I didn't budge, Puffy **flapped** his fins. "Let's go! She's looking all over for you!"

"Who is **she**?" I asked.

"SCORCHER — you know, the Ancient One with Eyes of Fire, the WORST WITCH in the Kingdom of Fantasy," he replied.

Now I was confused. I had thought Cackle was the worst witch in the Kingdom of Fantasy.

Impatiently, Puffy explained that SCORCHER was even more evil than Cackle. "Basically, she's Cackle's boss," he started to say, when suddenly he yelled, "Watch out! Behind youuuuuu!"

I looked over my shoulder and **froze**. It was a shark! Behind it I saw another six **sharks**! Puffy whipped around and **ZIPPED** off to hide behind a rock. Terrified, I swam after him, screaming, "Wait for me!"

I hid just in time. The sharks were getting closer — their **pointy** teeth gleamed. I pictured my best suit being **RIPPED** to shreds and started mourning its loss.

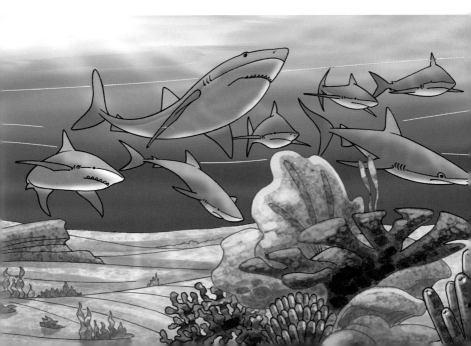

I was so busy thinking about my suit, I didn't realize the sharks had left.

"I bet you my **gills** she sent them after you!" Puffy said, interrupting my thoughts.

"Wh-why me?" I stammered.

Puffy sighed and rolled his eyes. "Why don't you already know this?" he complained. But he informed me that I had been called to the **KINGDOM OF FANTASY** to fulfill something called the ANCIENT GEMSTONE PROPHECY. Scorcher did not want the prophecy to be fulfilled, so she was after my fur!

"Now, I'm taking you to Coral Academy, the underwater fairy school. *Coraline*, the headmistress, will explain the rest," Puffy concluded.

I followed him past colorful reefs until we reached an enormouse **pink** coral castle!

CORAL ACADEMY

CORAL ACADEMY

A fairy was waiting for us. She had long **red** hair that *SWIRLED* around her like a cloud. She wore a silky red dress dotted with seashells and a **sparkling** crown on her head.

"Welcome to **CORAL ACADEMY**," the fairy said, waving her glittering wand. "I am Coraline."

The fairy seemed friendly, but who knew? After

CORALINE

Coraline is the headmistress of Coral Academy, the school for fairies. Gentle but firm, she knows how to get her students to respect her. She always keeps an eye on them — otherwise they would get into lots of mischief!

learning about Scorcher, I didn't know what to think!

I decided I should stay on her **GOOD SIDE**, so I said, "I am honored to be of service to you, Headmistress Coraline."

Then I tried to bow, but instead I tripped on a shell and landed in a pile of ſeaweed! I turned as red as a **LOBSTER**. I could see Puffy stifling a giggle.

Luckily, Coraline didn't seem to notice. "Follow me," she said.

Puffy
A noble fish from the Finn dynasty, Puffy is a talking puffer fish who is very friendly. He's not a great swimmer, but knows how to defend himself from large predators. He's a loyal aide to Coraline.

Coraline took us through a maze of hallways. Little **FAIRIES** flitted all around. Some carried schoolbooks and some seemed to be practicing spells. A chair with a fairy on it flew toward the ceiling, dishes **crashed** to the floor, and potions **BREWED** in pots.

As we passed by, the fairies stopped to stare and whisper among themselves.

"**WHO'S THAT?**" I heard one ask.

"He looks like that famous knight," another added.

"What was his name? Oh yeah — **Sir Geronimo of Stilton**," a third declared.

At this point all of the fairies were staring.

"Do you think it's really **HIM**?" someone asked.

"If it is, then he is the one who will make the **ANCIENT GEMSTONE PROPHECY** come true!" another answered.

Just then, a bold fairy swam up to me. "So, what's your name?" she asked.

Before I could answer, Puffy slapped a fin over

Shhh!

my mouth and said, "He's . . . my cousin!"

At this, the little fairy **narrowed** her eyes. Of course she knew Puffy was lying. I mean, when was the last time you met a **mouse** and a *fish* who were related?!

"No, seriously," the fairy pressed. "Who are you?"

I wasn't sure **why** Puffy didn't want anyone to know my identity, but I had been on enough of these **adventures** to know when to keep my mouth shut.

Luckily, Coraline CHiMED in before the silence got too awkward. "Gabby Waterwings! Don't you know it is rude to pester our guests?" she reprimanded. Then, with a wave of her wand, she ordered all the fairies back to their classrooms.

The fairies floated away, leaving behind them a trail of BUBBLES.

After the last fairy had disappeared down the hallway, the headmistress turned to me. "I know you are Sir Geronimo of Stilton, the **BRAVE** and *famous* knight, but from now on, we need to keep your name a secret. Now, please follow me. I'll explain everything to you when we reach my secret shell," she whispered.

Then she floated off, her silk clothes swaying behind her and her rosy wand glowing.

WANDA

Wanda is Coraline's magic wand. In addition to all of her magical powers, Wanda can also give advice and warn others about potential dangers.

THE ANCIENT GEMSTONE PROPHECY

Coraline floated on and on, turning **right** then **left** then **right** again. It felt like we were going in circles! Suddenly the fairy came to an abrupt stop. I kept going, and — BONK! I smacked my head on an enormouse **pink** shell.

Oh, how embarrassing!

Coraline touched the shell with her wand and slowly it opened. She motioned for us to follow her inside, and the shell closed behind us.

"Wow!" I breathed, looking around. The place was breathtaking! It **shimmered** with a delicate **pinkish glow**.

The fairy sat in a pink armchair and offered me some cookies. I was so ***hungry*** I popped three in my mouth. Big mistake! The cookies

were filled with **slimy** seaweed! I didn't want to be rude, so I politely **choked** them down.

Luckily, I was distracted from their taste when the fairy began talking. She said that she knew who I was. She'd heard of my many **BATTLES** with the wicked Queen of the Witches, and how I had helped Queen Blossom and **saved** the Kingdom of Fantasy.

"It is in her name that I once again ask for your **HELP**," the fairy said.

"Of course," I agreed. What else could I say? I am a gentlemouse.

"You will be fighting **SCORCHER**. She is the evil Empress of Witches. She has a heart of **poison**," Coraline went on.

I gulped. In addition to being a gentlemouse, did I mention I am also a **scaredy-mouse**?

"Is she really that **wicked**?" I asked.

Coraline nodded. "Yes, she is that wicked. But

she wasn't always that way. Before she turned evil, she was entrusted with the **RoyaL Ruby**, a gemstone with enormous powers. Now she is after the **Royal Sapphire**, another gemstone with even greater powers. Luckily, the sapphire is currently guarded by **AZUL**, the King of Sapphire City. But if Scorcher were able to get her hands on the sapphire, the entire Kingdom of Fantasy would be in terrible danger!"

"How **AWFUL**!" I exclaimed. "Someone must stop her!"

How awful!

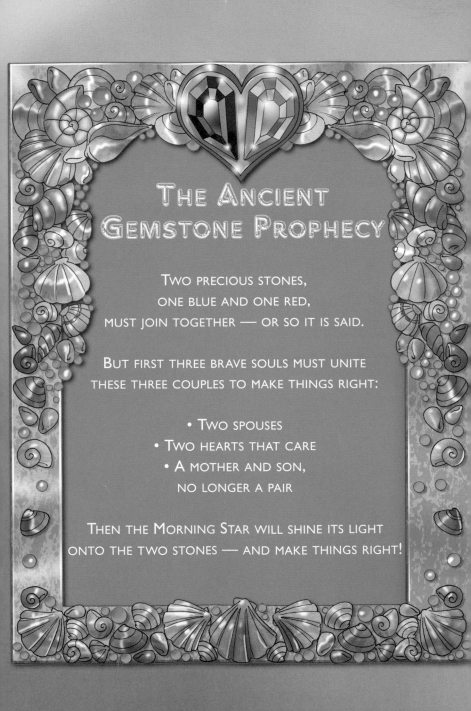

THE ANCIENT GEMSTONE PROPHECY

TWO PRECIOUS STONES,
ONE BLUE AND ONE RED,
MUST JOIN TOGETHER — OR SO IT IS SAID.

BUT FIRST THREE BRAVE SOULS MUST UNITE
THESE THREE COUPLES TO MAKE THINGS RIGHT:

- TWO SPOUSES
- TWO HEARTS THAT CARE
- A MOTHER AND SON,
  NO LONGER A PAIR

THEN THE MORNING STAR WILL SHINE ITS LIGHT
ONTO THE TWO STONES — AND MAKE THINGS RIGHT!

Coraline nodded. "Yes, it is awful — and that's why we need you! The only way we can stop this **CATASTROPHE** is to make sure the ANCIENT GEMSTONE PROPHECY is fulfilled. Once the two stones are united, peace will come."

"But how can I help?" I asked.

"You can help because you are one of the **three brave souls** the prophecy speaks of!" the fairy announced.

> YOUR TASK WILL BE TO BRING THE TWO TREASURED GEMSTONES TOGETHER AND ENSURE THAT THE STAR OF THE MORNING STRIKES THEM BOTH AT THE SAME TIME.

"To achieve this, you must:

1. Find Scorcher's castle, which is hidden in **Rotten Valley**.
2. Take the powerful **ruby** away from Scorcher.
3. Bring it to Shining Moon Mountain, where Azul guards his enormous *sapphire*.

④ **UNITE** the three couples that were unjustly divided."

I *chewed* my whiskers. This sounded very complicated and very *dangerous*. I wanted to suggest that maybe I wasn't the mouse for the job, but Coraline kept on talking.

"You should also know that Scorcher is already gathering her **army** together to snatch the **Royal Sapphire**. So you must act quickly!" she said.

My paws began to shake. When I had encountered Cackle's army, I had been scared out of my fur!

Then the fairy added, "Oh, and just so you are prepared, Scorcher is *ten times more wicked* than Cackle. She is said to have a heart as hard as

a rock, the breath of a smoky volcano, and a taste for raw mice."

I turned as pale as mozzarella.

"Are you okay?" Coraline asked, concerned.

I didn't want to look like a scaredy-mouse, so I squeaked, "Oh no, I'm fine! Better than ever!"

The fairy clapped her hands. "That's wonderful. You are so BRAVE, Sir Knight!" she said.

I started to straighten my tie but my paws were SHAKING so hard I practically choked myself.

"Brave, my fin," Puffy whispered in my ear with a chuckle.

Gasp...

THE GIFTS OF
THE FAIRIES

"I have good news for you," Coraline announced. "You won't be alone on this adventure. Along the way you will find two more **brave heroes** who will help you — that's what the prophecy says. But be careful: It's up to you to recognize them. Beware of false friends. . . ." she warned.

Immediately, I felt a little better.

"Great! Two **heroes** to help me. Not that I need help or anything . . ." My voice trailed off.

Coraline was staring at me closely. Was my fur a **mess**? Did I have food in my teeth?

"I just realized that we must give you a disguise, so that Scorcher will not recognize you," she said. "I've got it! You'll make believe you're a **troubadour***!"

* **troubadour**: *a traveling poet-musician in the Middle Ages*

"Great idea," Puffy agreed. Then he stared at me quizzically. "A troubadour must have a nice voice. Can you *sing*, Sir Knight?" he asked.

"Um, well, sort of — I mean, maybe . . ." I babbled.

"Okay, let's hear it!" commanded the little fish.

So I cleared my throat and sang a scale:

"Do re mi fa sol la ti . . . !"

The little fish covered his ears with his fins. Coraline's eyes opened **WIDE**.

Something told me they weren't impressed.

"I have an idea," said the fairy, leading the way back toward Coral Academy. We stopped in a hallway before three pink doors.

Coraline turned to me and said, "You will be facing many dangers on your adventure, Sir Knight. But the FAIRIES are here to help. We have important *gifts* to give you. Please use them wisely."

Then she knocked on the first little door, which was labeled *Melody: The Fairy of Music*.

A melodious musical voice sang out, "Coooooome iiiiiin!"

The door swung open, and I saw a fairy playing a golden harpsichord*.

She was dressed in a **BLUE** gown decorated with MUSICAL NOTES. Her hat had a long veil dotted with treble clefs.

"Whaaat maaay I doooo for yoooooou?" she warbled harmoniously.

Coraline sighed. "We need to disguise this rodent as a traveling singer, but alas . . ."

"Say no more," Melody **CHIRPED**. Then she instructed me to sing.

* **harpsichord**: *an instrument resembling a piano that produces sound by plucking a string when a key is pressed*

MELODY

THE FAIRY OF MUSIC

Lady of the Melodious Kingdom, Queen of Harmonious Songs, and Princess of Minuets, Melody teaches singing at Coral Academy.

I had hardly uttered one full note when Melody clamped a hand over my mouth. "I can hear the problem!" she exclaimed.

"What is it?" I asked.

The fairy chuckled. "The problem, my dear mouse, is that you can't sing to save your life! But don't worry, I can fix everything," she assured me.

She picked up a little **GOLDEN** harp and whispered to it. Immediately, the strings began to **vibrate** and the harp began to sing in a beautiful voice, "*Do re mi fa sol la ti do!*"

The first gift from the fairies!

HARPER

"This is **HARPER**," said the fairy. "She can sing for you, while you lip-synch! You know, move your mouth as if you were singing, without making any sound. Problem solved!"

I looked at Harper, who **winked**.

"No worries," she said. "I've got your back or, er, your **VOCAL CORDS**."

Next Coraline knocked on the second little door, which read **Novella: The Fairy of Literature**.

A fairy with hair as dark as ink opened the door. She wore a long red dress embroidered with *gold* letters of the alphabet.

NOVELLA
THE FAIRY OF LITERATURE
Lady of Beloved Books, Queen of the Story Kingdom, and Princess of Invented Tales, she teaches fairy literature at Coral Academy. Don't mess with her — she is very strict!

"Please come in," said the fairy, ushering us into a room filled floor to ceiling with **BOOKS**.

I was in heaven! I love **BOOKS**! I love writing them, reading them, and even SMELLING them! Books have the most comforting scent!

Anyway, where was I? Oh, yes. Once we were seated, Novella said, "I am told you are an **EXTRAORDINARY** writer, so I would like to give you an **EXTRAORDINARY** gift you can use to write about your adventures."

She pulled open a large drawer in her desk. "These are my **EXTRAORDINARY** pens," she said. "Please choose your favorite."

All of the feather pens were jumping up and

Rosy

Charmer

Spunky

Sunny

Sassy

Curly

down in their inkwells. "Pick me! PiCK ME!" they cried.

One of the pens was shouting louder than the others. Intrigued, I asked the fairy, "What's her name?"

Novella smiled. "That one is **Honor**, a descendant of an ancient family of pens that only write the **truth**," she said.

"That's right! My ink won't tell a **lie**," the pen agreed. "You'll see — we'll be perfect together!"

"Okay," I said, picking up the excited pen.

The second gift from the fairies!

Honor

Finally, Coraline knocked on the third little door, which read *Lovely: The Fairy of Beauty and Transformations.*

The door opened and we found ourselves in a room filled with the **sweet perfume** of roses. A beautiful fairy moved gracefully toward us. She wore a simple pink gown decorated with flowers, and her golden hair was held back by two rose barrettes.

"Hello, my name is *Lovely.* I hear you're in need of a transformation, which is my specialty!" she proclaimed.

LOVELY

THE FAIRY OF BEAUTY AND TRANSFORMATIONS

Princess of the Changing Kingdoms and Queen of Magical Makeovers, Lovely teaches beauty spells and transformations at Coral Academy.

She stuck me in front of a mirror, then stared at me thoughtfully. "Hmm, let's see. I could make your ears **larger**, but that would just look weird . . . or maybe I could dye your fur **RED** . . . nah, you'd look like a clown. Or how about a beard . . ." she murmured.

She began **WAVING** her wand as she chanted:

> *"Grow a beard*
> *that's long and white,*
> *one that's seen*
> *by day or night!"*

Instantly, my chin began **itching**. When I looked in the mirror, I screamed. I looked like RIP VAN WHISKERS, the legendary mouse who fell asleep for twenty years. My beard was down to my knees!

"Okay, let me try something else," said the fairy,

waving her WAND again and mumbling:

> "Vanish, beard, from the mouse's face.
> Handlebar mustache,
> take its place!"

Puffy snorted. "He looks ridiculous!"

So the fairy waved her wand again, CHANTING:

> "Curly hair, wild and free,
> adorn this mouse for all to see!"

Before I could squeak, curly blond locks **tumbled** down my shoulders.

"All wrong," Lovely muttered, sizing me up.

Then she **snapped** her fingers. "I've got it!" she exclaimed, floating to her bookshelf and pulling down a huge book. She flipped to a page that read "troubadour disguise," and, waving her WAND, chanted:

"This troubadour's cape will be the charm
to keep you safe and free from harm!"

This time when I looked in the mirror, I smiled. I didn't look like a mouselet playing dress-up anymore. I was wearing a simple **GRAY** tunic and **GREEN** cape. I put my new pen and harp into the bag around my shoulder.

Coraline smiled. "You are ready for your *secret mission*. From now on you will be known as the *Music Mouse*," she announced.

The third gift from the fairies!

A TROUBADOUR'S DISGUISE

BEWARE OF FALSE FRIENDS!

Coraline snapped her fingers and a fish that looked like a huge dark sheet swam to her side. It was an enormouse **MANTA RAY**. The fish bowed, making its flat and smooth body a shimmering wave in the water, then shouted, "Rayleen at your service!"

I cautiously mounted its back and held on to two reins of braided algae.

Before we took off, the fairy warned me, "**Be careful!** Always keep to the main road, and don't stop until you reach Shining Moon Mountain. Don't look for shortcuts, don't tell your SECRETS to strangers, and . . . beware of false friends! Friends should be judged not by what they say, but by what they do."

"Don't worry!" I said as we took off. After all, how hard could it be to tell a **real** friend from a **false** friend?

I was more worried about falling off the giant manta ray!

RAYLEEN

Descended from the noble family of Ray, Rayleen is a giant manta ray. Silent and cunning, she escorts visitors from one end of the kingdom to the other and is often given the most important and dangerous missions.

Good-bye!

Still, I put on a **BRAVE** face, though I was a nervous wreck. I didn't want Coraline to worry about me!

Rayleen swam farther and farther up toward the surface. The sea around me became **CLEARER** and clearer until we hit the surface and emerged.

The fish deposited me on a rock.

"Good luck, *Music Mouse*," she said with a wink of one of her protruding eyes. Then she *plunged* back into the sea and disappeared.

Immediately, I wished I could return to the

Do you mind?!

magical world beneath the sea where it was nice and safe and there were no **EVIL** witches around. But I had no choice. Rats!

I took off down a path between two trees with Harper and Honor hopping along beside me. Eventually we reached the main road, a wide path paved with gray **STONES**. There I spotted a sign written in the FANTASIAN ALPHABET. Can you translate it?*

*You can find the Fantasian alphabet on page 311.

I translated the sign. It said, "**Rotten Valley**." I gulped. This was it. Rotten Valley was where I would find the evil witch Scorcher's castle. Oh, how I wished I was home in my nice **COZY** mouse hole!

I guess Harper could tell I was nervous, because just then she began singing loudly to cheer me up.

"**La, la, la, la, la, la, la!**" she trilled.

"Do you mind? I am trying to enjoy the peaceful quiet," Honor huffed.

"I sing because it makes me HAPPY," Harper replied.

"Well, it makes me want to scream and write unhappy stories," the pen complained.

The two continued to **argue** for fifteen minutes until I couldn't take it anymore. Without a word, I picked them up and stuck them back into my bag.

"How **RUDE**!" they exclaimed together. But I ignored them and kept walking. I walked and walked and walked. By the time night fell, I was exhausted.

Finally, I came to an odd sign which read, "This way to the **INN OF THE WEARY TRAVELER**."

For a second, I remembered Coraline's warning to always stay on the **main road**. But the sign seemed to be written just for me.

I mean, it was an inn (and I needed a place to sleep), it was for **travelers** (and I was a traveler), and it was specifically for those who were **weary** (and I was very weary and tired!).

Besides, I would go right back to the **main road** after I'd had a good night's rest. So, without another thought, I headed **toward** the inn.

THE INN OF THE
WEARY TRAVELER

It was long past **SUNSET** when I finally reached the inn. Inside I could hear loud singing and **terrifying** noises. I **FROZE**. Was it safe? On the one paw, I was scared out of my wits, but on the other paw, I was so, so tired.

Finally, I made up my mind. I had to get some

sleep or I'd be one **CRANKY** mouse. I pulled the hood down over my eyes, took a deep breath, and went in. As soon as I entered, I wanted to run back outside. The inn was filled with the most **HORRIFYING** creatures I had ever seen!

There were enormouse monsters with **PIERCING** eyes and tentacles instead of arms, and groups of witches with **SCREECHING** cackles. There was also a group of Heartless Horsemen, who I know are very loyal to **Cackle**, the Queen of the Witches. In the corner I even spotted a group of large, **HISSING** snakes. I watched in amazement as the biggest one **slithered** up to the innkeeper. He had a gold coin between his fangs. The innkeeper took the coin, then

brought out a steaming bowl of soup for the snakes.

I tried to **sneak** in without being noticed, but the innkeeper grabbed me by the tail.

"Hey, you! Who are you, and what do you want?" he barked.

So much for blending in. "Ahem, my name is M-M-Music M-M-M-Mouse and I'm a poor **troubadour**," I stammered. "I don't have any money, but I could **SING** for your customers if you'd like."

The innkeeper stared at me so hard I thought for sure he knew I was lying. But then he said, "Okay, sit there and start playing. And you better sing **WELL**, or you'll be sorry!"

"Well, um, yes, of course — I mean, I understand — that is, don't worry . . ." I babbled, frantically **yanking** Harper out of my bag.

"Hey, what's the **BIG** idea? I was sleeping," she whined. But when I explained that we had an audience and I needed her to play, she brightened.

"Audiences *love* me!" she whispered.

I looked out at the crowd of monsters, who were now all staring at me **menacingly**. I sure hoped Harper was right!

Then I opened my mouth, and she began to sing a soft sweet song. Unfortunately, we weren't a HIT. Though we did get HIT with tomatoes, fish, half-eaten carrots, and other types of flying food. What a disaster!

"What's with the *sappy* stuff? Sing something else!" the crowd shouted. "We want monsters, blood, and battles!"

The only one who didn't complain was a *scraggly*-looking fox, who just stared at me strangely.

"I have never been so **INSULTED** in all my life!" Harper whispered.

Still, I convinced her to try singing another song. This one was about a brave knight and a princess, but there were also some **WICKED** witches, ogres, poisonous plants, and a slew of battling monsters.

The crowd went wild. They LOVED it!

Many of the monsters threw gold coins at me. I quickly picked them up and shoved them in my pocket because I thought they might come in handy.

The harp whispered in my ear, "I want half, okay? I **sang** the song!"

"What about me?" protested Honor. "I **wrote** the song!"

"*Quiet!*" I whispered, just in time — right then, the innkeeper appeared at my side.

He was holding a bowl of **slimy** fish soup that had a swarm of flies **hovering** over it. He slammed it on the table along with a moldy piece of bread and mug of **CLOUDY** water, muttering, "You earned your grub, Music Mouse."

I know it sounds **gross**, but I slurped the rancid soup right up, and gnawed on the stale bread. I couldn't help it. I was starving!

As I began to eat, I had the feeling *someone* was watching me. . . .

MAY I JOIN YOU?

I turned and saw the same **fox** who I had noticed earlier staring at me again. When I looked closer, I realized he wasn't a fox at all. He was actually a coyote.

He was **tall** and **SKINNY**, with sharp ribs beneath his mottled fur. He wore a satchel across his shoulders that had a dirty piece of lace, some **scruffy** ribbons, and a cheap-looking necklace hanging out. He had a **SHARP** face and pointy ears. One of his ears appeared to have been bitten half off, and his tail was **crooked** as if it had been broken and badly fixed. He came toward me leaning on a wooden stick.

"May I join you?" he asked. "You look out of place among all of these monsters. I can tell you are a **ReFineD** traveler like me."

I hesitated. Coraline had warned me not to **truʃt** strangers. But the coyote seemed harmless, and I didn't want to be rude. So I nodded.

The coyote stuck his paw out and said, "My name is Rex Ranger Redtail but everyone just calls me Ranger for short."

Slurp!

He lowered his voice, "Isn't this the **scariest** place? There are so many monsters! And who knows how many are spies for the witch?"

"You mean **SCORCHER**?" I asked.

He nodded and whispered, "Exactly! Rumor has it she's looking for someone who is on an **IMPORTANT** mission. Know anything about it?"

I lowered the hood on my face. My fur had turned beet **RED**!

"I don't know anything. I'm just a poor **troubadour**," I mumbled.

The coyote stared at me for a long time and

said, "Oh, of course — I'm sure you don't know anything. You're just a **POOR** singer, and I'm just a **POOR** door-to-door salesman who earns his living selling lace and cheap jewelry. . . ."

He opened his bag and showed me some lace handkerchiefs and flashy fake jewelry.

"Want to buy anything? I'll give you a discount," he said.

I took one of the gold coins and offered it to him. I had no idea what I would do with the handkerchief or cheap jewelry, but I felt bad. It was obvious this poor traveler was down on his **LUCK**.

The coyote grabbed the coin and cried, "Oh, thank you so much, *generous* stranger! May fate reward you for your good heart!"

We chatted for a little until my eyes grew heavy. I was pooped!

I said good night and dragged myself to the STRAW PILE the innkeeper had made for me in the stable. I was so tired, I hardly noticed the stinky smell. Well, okay — I noticed it, and thought about suggesting to the innkeeper he invest in some **AIR FRESHENERS**, but then I fell asleep.

At dawn the following morning, I headed for the main road. The sun was **SHINING** and I was glad to be away from the stinky stable.

The harp *played* and the pen had slipped behind one of my ears to enjoy the scenery. I smiled, staring up at the clear blue sky. Then, suddenly, a *shadow* loomed before me.

"**ACK!**" I squeaked, taking a step back.

But when I looked up, I realized it was only Ranger, the coyote from the inn.

"Sorry, friend, didn't mean to **scare** you! I was just so excited to see you!" he said with a grin. "Wanna walk together? There are lots of **thieves** around here. By the way, not to be too nosy or anything, but where are you headed?"

I hesitated. I knew Coraline had warned me about trusting **strangers** and mentioning the search for the **GEMSTONES** . . . but Ranger wasn't really a stranger anymore, right? I had met him just the night before, but he seemed like he might turn out to be a good **friend**.

"Silence is a good thing. Don't **spill** all your secrets," Harper sang in a soft whisper.

But it was too late. I had made up my mind.

I told Ranger where I was headed, and he clapped his paws.

"What a coincidence!" he exclaimed. "I just

happen to be headed to **Rotten Valley**, too! This is perfect! We can **TRAVEL** together!"

Then, lowering his voice, Ranger whispered, "Rotten Valley is a very dangerous place. I heard it is popular with bandits. Plus, did you know that somewhere hidden in Rotten Valley is the castle of the INCREDIBLY EVIL witch Scorcher?"

Instantly, my fur turned pale. Oh, why did everyone have to talk about how INCREDIBLY EVIL Scorcher was?!

Ranger must have noticed my distress, because he patted my shoulder.

"Don't be afraid, my friend. I know all the safe roads," he assured me.

Being the **scaredy-mouse** that I am, I was glad to have the coyote by my side.

After three days of traveling we reached a huge gate that seemed to have been struck by a bolt of *LIGHTNING*.

1. THE FOREST OF SEVEN
   THIEVES
2. BREAKDOWN BOULEVARD
3. THE ENCHANTED ROSE
   GARDEN
4. FLOWERING CASTLE
5. STONE BRIDGE

6. BOILING POND
7. QUICKSAND SWAMPS
8. WAILING GHOST GORGE
9. PIERCING SPEARS
10. ALLIGATOR PIT
11. THUNDERING ROCK
12. WARLOCK WELL

ROTTEN VALLEY

THE BAND OF SEVEN THIEVES

I stared at the patched-up gate with a sinking feeling of dread in my stomach. I don't know what I was expecting the entrance to a place called **Rotten Valley** to look like, but a **WeLcome SiGn** or a new paint job would have been nice. Or maybe even some **FLOWERING** shrubs nearby. My great-aunt Tinyrat lives in an old apartment, but she always puts two little pots of flowers at her front door, and it *cheers* the place right up.

I was still thinking about flowers when Ranger suggested we leave the main road and take a shortcut through the woods.

"I heard that this path is a lot *FASTER* and **SAFER**," he insisted.

At first, I hesitated. Coraline had warned me about taking shortcuts. But Ranger said, "Don't be afraid. **TRUST ME** — it will be a lot faster!"

I couldn't wait to get out of that creepy forest, so I said, "Okay."

The minute we were off the main road, I regretted my decision. **DARK** trees blocked any remaining light as dusk approached. And when

I looked closer at the trees, I realized something. We were in a **PETRIFIED** forest! The trunks, branches, and even the leaves of the trees were all made of **slone**. The only things not petrified were the bramble bushes covered with thorny, poisonous leaves.

CHEESE NIBLETS! THIS PLACE WAS A NIGHTMARE!

Still, what could I do? It was too late to turn around. Besides, my mission was to find Scorcher's castle and get my paws on the treasured **Royal Ruby**. Too bad there was no sign of the castle.

Soon it was nightfall. Oh, how I hate the dark!

"Ahem, are you sure this is the right road?" I asked the coyote.

"Of course!" yelped Ranger, pushing past another **CROOKED**, **THORNY** bush. But as I stared at the bush, a terrible thought hit me. The walking stick Ranger was using looked exactly like it was from a thorny bush! Had he been here before?

"Um, what's the name of this forest?" I asked with a nervous laugh.

"We're in the Forest of Seven Thieves," he chuckled.

How many thieves
are hidden in the
forest?

Ha, ha, ha!

Answer: There are more than 6. Turn the page to find out who the seventh is!

He had barely finished talking when six scary-looking creatures JUMPED out from behind the thorny bushes.

"And this is the BAND OF SEVEN THIEVES!" Ranger continued. He began to chant:

"**UGHS**, the troll with bugs,
Blight, the rebel knight,
SNEER, the ogre of fear,

THE BAND OF SEVEN THIEVES

I'm stinky!

I'm a traitor!

Blight

I'm wicked!

UGHS

SNEER

GLOOM, the drummer of doom,
CRASS, the gnome with no class,
NED, the elf of dread."

"B-but there are only s-s-six thieves," I stammered. At which point, Ranger bowed and said, "Allow me to formally introduce myself, **fRieND**. My full name is Ranger, the coyote of **danger**!"

Then, before I could scream, they tied me up and carted me off!

NOT BAD?

As if things weren't bad enough, I could hear Honor complaining away in my bag. "I told him not to go off the main road. But nooooo . . . no one ever wants to trust a PEN anymore! We're too OLD-FASHIONED!" she sulked.

Meanwhile the coyote was jumping *up* and down excitedly.

Help!

"Can you believe I got the rat, boss?" he babbled to the knight, who must have been the leader of the motley crew. "Scorcher will definitely **REWARD** us when we hand him over!"

They were taking me to Scorcher?! I gulped. How do I get myself into these **terrifying** predicaments? I mean, I try to avoid **scary** things . . . like spiders and roller coasters. In fact, the last time I got on a roller coaster I **screamed** for twenty minutes before the ride even started!

I was so busy **SOBBING**, I hardly noticed the knight rummaging through my bag.

"What do we have here?" he said, pulling out the harp and the pen. "This looks like a pretty nice harp, and this is a decent-looking pen. **Not bad**. Not bad at all."

"Not bad?" Harper groused. "I'm made of solid **GOLD**!"

"Not bad? I'm an **antique** feather pen!" Honor added.

Before they could go on, the knight shoved them back into the bag and continued walking. I tried not to think about where we were going and what the **evil witch** would do to me once we got there. It wasn't easy.

As the gang walked, they talked about the witch, her evil ways, and my fate. Basically, all of the things I was trying so hard not think about!

"I think the witch will pay us well for a CHUBBY mouse like this," commented the ogre.

"Well, I think we should roast him and make a tasty soup for ourselves," the troll suggested.

"Yuck! I wouldn't eat it if you paid me!" the drummer balked.

Pretty soon the gang was so busy arguing that they didn't see the knight on horseback galloping right for us!

The knight was dressed all in **BLUE** and rode on an enormouse white stallion. He wielded his long, SHARP sword and shouted, "Surrender, crooks! I am Blue Rider, defender of the weak, and hero to the helpless and hopeless!"

On hearing those words, the thieves dropped the pole I was strapped to and VANiSHED into the woods. I crashed to the ground.

Youch! That hurt!

At first I was happy, but then I saw the knight **racing** toward me with his sword drawn!

"*HOOOOOOLD STILLLLLLLLL!*" he screamed.

I couldn't believe it! I had thought this knight was on my side. He had said he was a hero to the helpless and the hopeless. Who was more helpless and hopeless than me?

I was sure he was about to skewer me like a mouse-kebab. I squeezed my eyes shut . . . and heard a strange sound. *ZIP!*

The sword never touched me as he sliced the rope that held me. I was free!

"You saved my life!" I squeaked.

"Of course," Blue Rider said matter-of-factly. "I am a hero. I am daring, courageous, and CHARMING. I am the best of the best!"

I coughed. I guess his mother never told him that it's not nice to **BRAG**.

The knight turned to leave, but a moment later he jumped off his horse and ran to the foot of an **OAK** tree. Then he started **shaking** the trunk of the tree like a lunatic.

"I see you! I see you!" he yelled, staring at the leaves.

I didn't see a thing. For a minute I wondered if Blue Rider might have gone a little cuckoo from all this **saving** lives business, but then a foot appeared from the leaves. A second later, the elf from the gang of thieves fell to the ground, took one look at the knight, and ran *shrieking* down the road.

Blue Rider **CLIMBED** back on his horse.

"Wait! Please don't leave me in this **CREEPY** forest! Take me with you," I cried.

"Sorry, mouse," answered the knight, "but I'm not a chaperone. I'm a **HERO**. I've got more lives to save."

Quickly, I came up with an idea. I told Blue Rider that I was a writer — I could write a story where he was the 𝔰𝔱𝔞𝔯.

"I am already a **STAR**," the knight said, insulted. But then he brightened.

"I know! You can write the story of my life. After all, I am the **BEST OF THE BEST**! Who wouldn't want to read about me?" he said.

What could I say? I had to get out of that **forest**, so I agreed.

Then I climbed on the back of the knight's horse, and we took off.

Blue Rider:
The Best of the Best!

THE MYSTERIOUS STORY OF BLUE RIDER

As we rode, Blue Rider wanted me to begin *writing*. So I clasped the horse's saddle strap with my teeth, flipped open my notebook with one paw, **GRIPPED** Honor with the other paw, and turned to a blank page with my tongue.

"Okay, I'm ready. You can start," I said. But with the saddle strap *clenched* between my teeth it sounded like, "Ohmmf mmrrmf rmmmmf."

Blue Rider starting **BLABBING** away.

"I was born in — nah, better not write that. I have to remain a MYSTERY! I was born on — nah, better not write that. I have to remain a MYSTERY! I'm the son of — nah, better not write that. I have to remain a MYSTERY!" he muttered.

I put down the pen. "Um, knight, if you don't tell me anything, how am I going to write the **STORY** of your life?" I asked.

Blue Rider **SNORTED** and replied, "I thought you said you were a writer! I mean, I'm a hero, and you don't see me complaining about **SAVING LIVES**, do you?" he said.

I gulped. I didn't want the knight to leave me behind in the **DARK** forest! So I said, "Uh, sure, no problem. I'll write something! I'll figure it out!"

So I began to write: *We don't know* **where** *he was born,* **WHEN** *he was born, or* **what** *family he belongs to, but it is supposed that he descends from a noble family, and . . .*

At this, Honor planted her pen tip on the **SHEET** of paper and refused to write any more.

"Oh, no! I can't do this. I write only the truth, remember?" she cried.

The harp peeked out of the bag and added her two cents.

"**OH, PLEASE!** You'll use any excuse to get out of doing some WORK! At least I did my part at the inn, singing and playing," she said.

I write only the truth!

"I'm not trying to get out of doing WORK!" Honor shot back. "Besides, I hate to break it to you, but your singing is NOTHING SPECIAL!"

Before I could stop them, the two were arguing. Could things get any worse?

Yes, yes they could. Right then, things went from BAD to really BAD. Blue Rider, who had apparently been listening to all of the arguing, stopped his horse.

"Mouse, if you can't get those two to stop **BICKERING** in thirty seconds, I'm going to turn this horse right around and drop you off where I found you in the woods!" he declared.

I cringed and buried my head in my notebook. Then I pretended to be writing furiously. As I did, I announced what I was pretending to write in a **LOUD** voice. "'Blue Rider is very daring, COURAGEOUS, and charming. He is braver than everyone in the entire Kingdom of Fantasy. He's the best of the best! He is also full of mystery, making him very mysterious. . . .'"

The knight continued riding across the **terrifying** Forest of Seven Thieves. A full moon shone overhead, in a spooky way.

As if things weren't scary enough, as we rode, we were attacked by packs of evil creatures.

I was pretty sure that Scorcher had sent them out to try and capture me! *Cheddar cheese fries, it was terrifying!*

The first to attack were seven **SNAKERS**, huge plants that tried to grab us with their clawed tendrils. Luckily the knight was able to zigzag his way past them. Next we were chased by **ROOTERS**, gigantic stone trees that tried to crush us. We escaped just in the nick of time!

After that we were surrounded by disgusting slurpers, monstrous anteaters who tried to slurp us up! They were followed by sixteen slithering **SNATS**, horrid creatures that were half snake, half bat. Finally, we fought off seventeen **gobblers**, goblins with a sweet tooth for mice!

Squeak!

SCORCHER'S EVIL ARMY

7 SNAKERS

Monstrous plants
with clawed,
snaking tendrils
used to squeeze
victims.

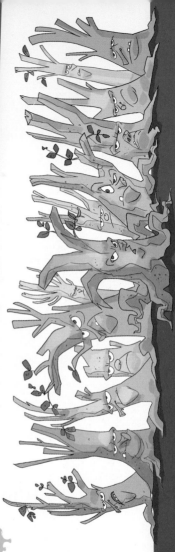

13 ROOTERS

Cruel, gigantic stone
trees that are skilled
in crushing anyone
with their gnarled,
grasping roots.

15 Slurpers

Creatures with long, anteater-like tongues that are covered with poisonous saliva.

16 Snats

Horrid creatures with the head of a bat and the body of a snake.

17 Gobblers

Goblins with a sweet tooth for crunching little mouse bones!

TENDERHEART'S SAD STORY

At DAWN, Blue Rider pulled his white stallion's reins to stop him. The horse looked tired.

Blue Rider jumped down. "My horse SNOWY is just like me — the best of the best!" he said, hugging the giant stallion. "Aren't you, Snowy-bowie? My little **horsey-worsey**!"

I stifled a laugh, but Snowy didn't seem to mind the baby talk. He happily nuzzled Blue Rider's neck. As the knight was brushing him, I noticed a *locket* slip out from underneath his coat. The locket popped open, revealing the picture of a BEAUTIFUL maiden.

"Is she your girlfriend?" I asked, curious.

For a minute the knight seemed to SMILE. He stared off into space and sighed dreamily. Ah, young **LOVE**! I was about to ask more questions when a strangely **SAD** expression came over the knight's face. In a flash, he shoved the *locket* back under his coat and said, "I don't want to talk about it."

Hmmm, I thought. Maybe the two were fighting. Maybe their horses didn't get along. Or maybe the maiden was tired of the knight **bragging** about himself all the time. (It *was* pretty annoying.)

By this time, it was late in the afternoon, and I was starving. Where was a good **pizzeria** when you needed one? Luckily, I managed to make a TASTY soup using just herbs.

The knight liked my soup so much, he decided to tell me about the *locket*. I grabbed the pen and began to write. . . .

♥ The Sad Story of Tenderheart ♥

Eighteen years ago, in the castle of King Cornflower, a little girl named Tenderheart was born. She had golden hair and blue eyes. But on Tenderheart's forehead was a special feature — a strange blue birthmark, shaped like a little heart.

All the fairies of the kingdom were called to interpret the sign, but no one could, until one day, her fairy godmother, the Fairy of Spring Flowers, came to the castle. She said the birthmark meant that the girl was destined to join her heart to the one who bore the same sign on his forehead. Together with this unknown hero and another chosen hero, Tenderheart would fulfill the Ancient Gemstone Prophecy, uniting that which was divided and bringing peace to the Kingdom of Fantasy.

Unfortunately, the evil witch Scorcher was determined to stop the princess. If the prophecy were fulfilled, she would lose her powerful Royal Ruby, which she loved even more than her own son.

And so, on Tenderheart's sixteenth birthday, the witch kidnapped the maiden and hid her in a secret location within the realm. From that day on, no one has been able to find Tenderheart — not even the unknown hero, who is still searching for her throughout the Kingdom of Fantasy.

I was glad when Blue Rider finally finished his story. Honor was so worked up over the tragic tale, she was **bawling** her eyes out, spilling tears all over the pages of my notebook.

"Sorry," she SOBBED.

I must admit, it was a touching story. Even I had a **tear** in my eye.

But I shook it off and **mopped** up the pages of my notebook. I didn't want to lose anything I had written. So far, this was the most

Boo hoo!

iɴteʀestiɴɢ part of Blue Rider's story. Little did I know things were about to get even more **iɴteʀestiɴɢ**. The knight pushed aside his bangs and showed me a birthmark on his forehead, admitting, "You might as well know, it's me."

It didn't take a **rocket scientist** to figure out what he meant. Yep, you guessed it — there on the knight's forehead was a birthmark shaped like a **little blue** heart!

Well, this explains a lot, I thought. Such as why the knight was so sad, why he was riding in **Rotten Valley**, and why he wore those **long**, *messy* bangs.

Suddenly, a BRILLIANT thought came to me. No, I hadn't figured out another hairstyle

to hide the knight's little forehead **secret**. I realized that Blue Rider must be one of the HEROES the prophecy spoke about!

Excitedly, I told the knight about the Ancient Gemstone Prophecy and how I had **promised** the fairies I would fulfill it. "If you help me complete the mission, we can search for Tenderheart along the way," I proposed.

The knight jumped to his feet. "Of course I'll help. After all, I am the BEST OF THE BEST!" he declared. "But what exactly do you need to do?"

"Sit down," I began. "This might take a while." Then I proceeded to explain the plan to locate Scorcher's castle, get the Royal Ruby, transport it to **Shining Moon Mountain** where the Royal Sapphire is located, bring the two **GEMS** together, and ensure that the Star of the Morning struck them both at the same time.

"Did you say Shining Moon Mountain?" Blue Rider asked after I finished. When I nodded he said, "I'm in!"

Then he jumped on his horse and said, "Come on! We have a mission to accomplish!"

It wasn't until we started riding that I remembered the other part of the strange and CONFUSING prophecy. . . . Something about uniting two **HEARTS**, two spouses, and a mother and son. Oh well — something told me this was going to be one **long** adventure, and I'd have plenty of time to fill Blue Rider in on everything eventually.

And so we continued riding through the woods until we came to a high thicket of red roses that gave off a sweet and mystifying scent. . . .

THE ENCHANTED ROSE GARDEN

THE ENCHANTED ROSE GARDEN

6

10

5

9

1. ROSEBUSH OF A THOUSAND PETALS
2. THE TRAVELER'S CLEARING
3. SINGING WOODS
4. WELL OF THE FORGOTTEN ROSES
5. SILVER PETAL LANE
6. FLOWERING PALACE OF THE LADY OF THE ROSE GARDEN
7. HOT POOL
8. STONE BRIDGE
9. RIVER OF FRAGRANT ROSES
10. TRAIL OF WILD ROSES

Don't Smell the Roses!

The towering thicket of red roses opened into an arch, forming a **shady**, fragrant covered passage.

"This is the Enchanted Rose Garden, where everything is possible — the very GOOD and the very bad," the knight murmured as we dismounted.

I looked around at the cheerful flowers, bright SUNNY skies, and singing birds. Compared to the dark, dreary woods we had just come from, this place looked like paradise. "What very bad things could happen to us here?" I said, bending down to sniff the roses.

Before I could take one whiff, Blue Rider pushed me away. "Don't smell the roses! They're

ENCHANTED! It's said that whoever inhales their perfume falls into a very deep sleep!"

When I looked skeptical, the knight went on. "I'm telling you, it's the truth! Plus, you better watch out for those thorns. If you get PRICKED, you will be changed into an insect!"

It was then that I noticed thousands of small, strange **insects** buzzing around the rosebush. Was it true? Were they really under a spell?

Just then Harper peeked out from my bag. "Blue Rider is right. Very GOOD and very bad things can happen in the Enchanted Rose Garden. There's even a song about it. Want me to *sing* it?" she said.

Humpf!

Quiet!

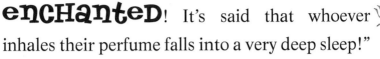

"Do you have to?" Honor complained.

But the harp was already **singing** at the top of her lungs. . . .

"Always give more than you take,
or your world may be at stake.
The Lady of the Garden is real — believe,
and precious gifts you will receive.
But if you cross her, woe to you:
You will surely end up blue!"

I was thinking about the _strange_ words of the song, when a golden carriage pulled by twelve **PRANCING** horses came into view. It was escorted by twelve soldiers on horseback. Each soldier wore a rich **RED** uniform with a plumed feather in his hat.

The carriage passed by us so closely it nearly ran us over!

"_**LOOK OUT!**_" I squeaked.

At that moment, a man dressed in _fancy_

clothes with gold rings on his fingers and a thick gold chain around his neck stuck his face out of the carriage window. "Look out yourselves, peasants!" he bellowed, looking down his nose at our simple clothes and worn shoes.

We watched as the carriage disappeared down the road. Hours later, we arrived in a clearing.

By this time, we were **exhausted** and decided to camp for the night.

Just then we heard what sounded like a starving animal devouring a meal. My fur **stood** on end. Was it a ravenous wolf? Or a wild boar?

I was about to run when I realized what it was. The rich traveler had set up camp next to us. He was seated at a formal dining table laden with food, and was *stuffing* his face.

As we watched, a poorly dressed old woman shuffled up to the table and asked the traveler for a bite to eat. "Please, Sire, I'm so HUNGRY and **thirsty**," she begged.

But the traveler just sneered, "Go away! The sight of you ruins my appetite!"

The old woman lowered her head. "I'm sorry, I won't bother you anymore!" she whispered. "May you receive a thousand times a thousand what you have given me. . . ."

"Can you believe that guy?" Harper cried.

"I'm going to write a story about him. I'll call it *The Rude Traveler*," Honor agreed.

"He should be ASHAMED of himself!" added the knight.

We invited the old woman to sit with us, and offered her half our food. I gave her my **WARM** cape and my last gold coin.

The old lady thanked us. "May you receive a thousand times a thousand what you have given me," she said.

Suddenly, the old woman was enveloped in a swirling wind of roses. In her place appeared a beautiful YOUNG woman with long blonde hair.

"I am the Lady of the Enchanted Rose Garden! And now, each will receive a thousand times a thousand of that which was given to me," she cried.

THE LADY OF THE ENCHANTED ROSE GARDEN

First the Lady turned to the rich traveler. She waved her arms and the table of food in front of him **vanished**. She waved again and the soldiers, horses, and even the traveler's **EXPENSIVE** clothes disappeared.

"What's going on?" he shrieked, hiding behind a bush.

Ack!

"You gave nothing, and so you will receive a thousand times a thousand of nothing, which is nothing," the Lady explained.

Then she turned

toward us. I **cringed**. Was I about to lose my shirt? How mortifying!

But when the Lady waved her arms this time, a table appeared, completely covered in **DeLiCiouS** foods and refreshing drinks.

The Lady said, "You gave me that which I needed. Therefore, *you will receive a thousand times a thousand of that which you need.*"

Then she handed me what looked like a pair of winged glasses.

"This is a **Focus Finder**," she explained. "It will show you anything that is hidden by magic in the kingdom."

The fourth gift from the fairies!

Focus Finder
A pair of magical glasses

I was so excited. Now we could find Scorcher's castle!

"I will also give you a vial filled with **Sapphire Water**, which is also called 'Fairies' Water,'" the Lady continued. "It's a concentration of **PURE LOVE**, capable of annihilating witches. And finally, I will give you a guide for your journey."

She lifted a hand and immediately a little bird with golden feathers (made out

The fifth gift from the fairies!

Sapphire Water

of real gold!) came to rest on it.

The bird stuck out his wing for me to shake. "CLEARFEATHERS, at your service! No, my feathers aren't CLEAR, but I can see everything very clearly. With me, you'll never get lost!" he chirped.

The Lady of the Garden smiled. "Yes, Clearfeathers is an **exceptional** guide who knows all the secret roads and HIDDEN paths. He

The sixth gift from the fairies!

CLEARFEATHERS
THE GOLDEN BIRD

will guard the precious Sapphire Water," she said.

Then she placed the vial around the bird's neck and disappeared in a Swirl of roses.

I carefully placed the **Focus Finder** in my bag. It was the perfect gift. How else would we find the evil witch?

It was late, so we decided to call it a night. I was so *tired*, I fell asleep in an instant. But all night long I dreamed someone or something was pulling at my clothes. . . . How strange!

The following day, Clearfeathers woke us at dawn, and I noticed he no longer had the vial of Sapphire Water around his neck. I asked him where he had hidden it, but he said mysteriously, **"In a secret place**."

We continued our journey, with the bird showing us the way until we arrived at the slimy **Suffering Swamps**.

WHO, ME?
SCARED?

I slipped through the opening of vines, which looked like tentacles reaching out to grab me, and trudged into the **SUFFOCATING** jungle. The ground was unstable and swampy and, to make matters worse, I had a weird feeling, like a thousand little wicked eyes were WATCHING me.

Right then, someone pulled my tail. "**AAAH!**" I squeaked, **jumping** a foot

Cheese niblets!

into the air and whipping around. There was no one behind me. Still, I was almost certain I had spotted something disappearing into the vines.

"You don't like scary places, do you, mouse?" Clearfeathers giggled. "You should see your face. You're as **PALE** as a ghost!"

"Who, me? Scared? Of course not," I mumbled, twisting my tail up in knots. "**YOUCH!**" I guess I wasn't fooling anyone.

Chirp!

"We can turn around if you want," Blue Rider offered. "I mean, not everyone can be daring, courageous, and brave like me. Oh, and charming, I almost forgot charming. Yep, I'm the best of the best, and furthermore . . ."

That's nothing!

As the knight bragged on and on about all of his amazing qualities, Clearfeathers circled overhead.

"Are you still **SCARED**, mouse?" he asked. "Because *this is nothing* compared to the scary things up ahead."

I shivered.

"Wh-what d-do you m-mean?" I stammered.

"Well, you could get sucked up into the **stinky swamp**, and be stuck there FOREVER with flies swarming over your head," he said.

As soon as Clearfeathers stopped talking, I took a step — and realized I was starting to get **sucked** up into the stinky swamp!

"Ahhh! I'm sinking!" I squeaked.

"Just sinking? Oh, that's nothing," the bird chirped. "You could be sinking and also have a million crabs gnawing at your fur."

Lucky for me, just then, Blue Rider stopped bragging and came to my RESCUE.

But as he was pulling me out of the muck I noticed something in the slime. The knight had lost his LOCKET, and it was about to get sucked under!

WATCH OUT FOR THE GORGE!

I grabbed it just in the nick of time. I held the LOCKET out to Blue Rider.

"What a save! *THANK YOU*, mouse," the knight said gratefully, slipping the gold chain back around his neck.

"I'm the one who should be thanking you. You **saved my life** again," I squeaked.

Blue Rider looked puzzled. "But of course, what else did you expect? I told you, mouse, I'm a **hero**. Saving lives is my job."

After resting for a few minutes we continued on our way, through the MISTY swamps. This time I tried to be extra careful. I didn't want to get sucked into another **stinky** pool of muck.

Soon we came to a humid tropical jungle. The MIST here was really heavy.

I put on the **Focus Finder** to try to look around for any sign of Scorcher's castle. Too bad it was so humid, though. The moisture **fogged** up the lenses, and I couldn't even see my own paw in front of my face!

Even so, I kept having the feeling that

Hmm . . .

SOMEONE was following us.

"Still scared, Mouse?" Clearfeathers chirped, noticing me shivering. "This is nothing. We could be attacked by a pack of **jungle zombies**. Or bitten by giant tarantulas!"

At this, Harper stuck her head out of my bag and shot the bird a look. "**Seriously?** Do you have to keep mentioning all of this **DOOM** and gloom? It's starting to get on my last chord!" she complained.

Before the bird could reply, Blue Rider suddenly grabbed me by the back of my cape and shouted, "**WATCH OUT FOR THE GORGE!**"

He had saved me! One more step and I would have **FALLEN** into a deep ravine hidden by the mist.

"You think this is bad? *This is nothing*," Clearfeathers chirped. "This is the **Great**

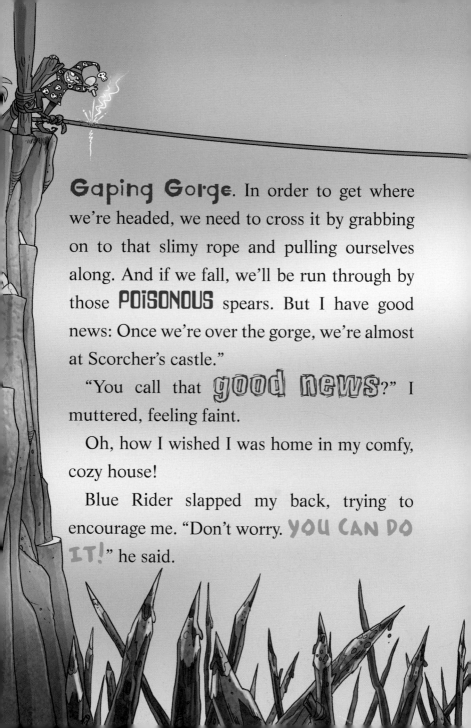

Gaping Gorge. In order to get where we're headed, we need to cross it by grabbing on to that slimy rope and pulling ourselves along. And if we fall, we'll be run through by those POISONOUS spears. But I have good news: Once we're over the gorge, we're almost at Scorcher's castle."

"You call that good news?" I muttered, feeling faint.

Oh, how I wished I was home in my comfy, cozy house!

Blue Rider slapped my back, trying to encourage me. "Don't worry. YOU CAN DO IT!" he said.

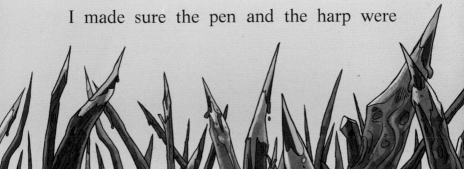

Aaaahh!

Now I was even more worried. Worried that the knight had just **broken** my back! I made a mental note to tell him to skip the back-slapping gesture next time and maybe stick with a pawshake.

"Watch me," the knight said, grabbing the rope. Moving like a **gymnast**, he crossed the gorge in minutes.

"Your turn!" he called.

My whiskers trembled and my teeth **CHATTERED** with fear. But I had no choice. I had to cross the gorge!

I made sure the pen and the harp were

tucked **SAFELY** into my bag, then began pulling myself across the rope bridge. Too bad I was such a nervous wreck, I was **shaking** like a leaf! I closed my eyes and tried to remember the relaxation techniques I had learned one time in a yoga class . . . something about picturing yourself near a **babbling** brook — or was it a peaceful sunny meadow?

I had managed to stop trembling when Blue Rider yelled, "You're doing it! Just don't look at the **poisonous** spears below you! Wow! They look deadly!"

Immediately, my eyes **popped** open and I looked up just in time to spy a little dark creature pouring something onto the rope.

The rope began **smoking**, and then it broke with a loud noise.

Crack!

The rope began to swing like a pendulum, and I smacked my head against the side of the rock. **Bam!**

My snout accidentally hit Clearfeathers and he also smacked his head on the **ROCK**. Luckily, I grabbed him before he fell into **EMPTINESS**.

And luckily Blue Rider grabbed the rope and pulled us both to safety.

What a nightmare!
What a **horror!**
What a **fright!**

Hold on!

WE ARE PIXIES
DRESSED IN BLACK!

Once we were all on solid ground again, we continued on our way.

"If I remember what the bird said, SCORCHER'S CASTLE should be right around here. Is that right, Clearfeathers?" the knight asked.

The bird looked confused.

"CLEARFEATHERS?" he chirped at us. "Who's Clearfeathers?"

Harper sprang out of the bag and *SCREECHED*,

Waaaah!

"What are you talking about?! *You're* Clearfeathers! That **CRACK** on the head must have knocked the sense out of you! Don't you remember anything?"

At that, Honor **burst** into

tears, spraying ink drops everywhere.

"**Waaaah!**" she sobbed. "Without the bird, we'll be lost here forever!"

I was about to start **SOBBING** along with the pen when I remembered something. "Wait a minute!" I squeaked. "We have the **Focus Finder**! It'll be easy to find Scorcher's castle!"

Smiling, I grabbed my pouch to get the glasses. Then I heard the horrible sound of broken glass.

Crunch! Crunch!

"Uh-oh," I squeaked.

"We're goners!" the harp screeched.

At least we had the vial with the **Sapphire Water** to use against the witch. But then I had a horrible thought.

We're goners!

"Where did you hide the magic **VIAL**?" I asked Clearfeathers.

The little bird stared at me. "What **VIAL**? I don't remember a vial!" he chirped.

We were in real **TROUBLE** now! Without the fairies' gifts and with a guide who had amnesia, how could we ever find Scorcher's castle? How could we ever **save** Tenderheart and fulfill the ancient prophecy?

Suddenly I saw something very strange. It was a small creature dressed in **black**, HOPPING

from one leaf onto another. I pretended I didn't see it.

Even though my heart was **HAMMERING**, I forced myself to keep walking while keeping an eye on the creature. He **LOOKED** like an elf no bigger than my paw, wearing odd clothes.

He seemed to be in a terrible huff as he **STAMPED** along after us. I tried to catch what he was muttering. It sounded like, "I can't believe they made it through! I should have turned them into stew! Now the witch will have my head! Or set Grizzle on me instead!"

I shuddered wondering who Grizzle was, but I didn't have much time to think about it because just then the little elf **LEAPED** away into some bushes. From the bushes we could hear very peculiar sounds.

We crouched down and saw a whole band of the little creatures. Their little black cloaks were

EMBROIDERED with white **skulls**.

Skulls?! Just my luck! Oh, why couldn't they be wearing little smiley faces or cheerful rainbows?

And as if the skulls on their clothes weren't bad enough, they also had little skulls hanging from the tips of their pointy hats. Inside the skulls were little **PeBBLeS** that clanked as they moved like mournful rattles. They were armed with small bows and arrows made of BONES.

The creatures rode on the backs of slobbering wild boars. As they rode they sang a scary song:

"We are pixies dressed in black!
We work for the witch, so watch your back!
We are cruel, greedy, and mean —
we're the meanest creatures you've ever seen!"

The pixies finished their song and burst out into such ghoulish **LAUGHTER**, it made all the flowers **WILT** and the birds stop singing.

SKULL PIXIES

Uniform: Black cloaks covered in embroidered skulls

Stone: Onyx

King: King Bones III

Where They Live: In Rotten Valley near Terror Castle (home of the evil Scorcher)

Currency: Pranky franc (they use the same money as the Kingdom of Pixies)

Spoken Language: Pixan

General Information: The Skull Pixies are the worst kind of pixies! They spy for Scorcher, the Empress of the Witches, and are loyal servants of her evil will. They're called Skull Pixies because they wear cloaks decorated with skulls, and bring terror and chaos wherever they go!

"Those are **Skull Pixies**. The worst kind of pixies," Blue Rider whispered. "They're Scorcher's spies. Rumor has it their hideaway is near Scorcher's castle, which means we're getting close. But we need to be careful. We don't want them picking up the *SCENT* of mouse."

Eek! I hoped they couldn't smell me! Good thing I had fallen into the swamp. . .

Huh?

But as we followed the Skull Pixies, something **BIZARRE** happened.

The Skull Pixies all began *galloping* toward a huge rock! They shouted:

"Beyond and yonder to the dark side!
The magic words we say with pride:
Not just a spell, not just a curse,
the secret works only in reverse!"

Then they disappeared into the rock!

Beyond and yonder . . .

BEYOND AND YONDER TO THE DARK SIDE . . .

We stared at the rock, dumbfounded.

Where had those little pixies disappeared to?

Just then I noticed that one skull pixie had been left behind. He shouted desperately, "Wait for me! Wait for me! I am here! Can't you see?"

It was the same little pixie that had been following us earlier. When he reached the rock, he stopped and whispered, "I wonder if I should tell the witch that I ran into a glitch. I couldn't stop the mouse's CREW, though I tried all I could do."

The pixie paced back and forth, looking worried. Finally, he muttered, "It's getting late. I

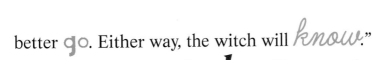

better go. Either way, the witch will *know*."

The pixie ran in **circles**. He seemed to be warming up. *It must be hard to run in those funny curly shoes*, I thought.

At last, he SPRINTED headlong into the rock, shouting:

"Beyond and yonder to the dark side!
The magic words we say with pride:
Not just a spell, not just a curse,
the secret works only in reverse!"

This time I noticed that an instant before the pixie hurled himself toward the wall, he murmured another word very **SOFTLY**. Then he *disappeared* into the rock, sinking like a knife into butter.

"I've got it!" I shouted, after he was gone. "I figured out how to follow them.

We have to say a **magic word** in order to soften the rock!"

Blue Rider turned to Clearfeathers.

"What lies beyond that rock?" he asked.

The bird held up his wings. "A movie theater? A **CANDY** store? A laser tag arcade? **Who knows?** Not me," he chirped, adding, "What'd you say my name was, again?"

There was nothing to do but to try something — anything. So I stood in front of the rock, and said, "Okay, okay now, the **magic word** could be . . . Skull Pixies?"

Don't know!

I pushed on the rock but it was as hard as ever. I tried again.

"**SKULLS?** Bats? **SCORCHER?** Empress? Witch's castle?"

But nothing happened. So I kept **spewing out** every word that came to mind:

"Wicked? Mean? Vicious? Cruel? Spell? Sorcery? Cauldron? Potion? Wart? Nose?"

Getting more discouraged, I tried, "Pointy hat? Evil charm? Flying broom? Black cat?"

Honor YAWNED and Harper climbed back into my bag. "Tell me when you get it. I'm taking a nap," she mumbled.

By now I, too, was feeling tired. How was I supposed to unite the treasured gemstones, find the things from the prophecy, and locate Tenderheart if I couldn't crack the secret code?

Discouraged, I sat down in the DIRT and began playing around with some little sticks. Without

thinking, I spelled out the word SCORCHER.

Suddenly, a **strong** wind picked up, **FLiPPiNG** the sticks around. When I stared back at the sticks, I realized some of the letters were mixed up. The little song the pixies had been singing came to mind. . . .

> *"Beyond and yonder to the dark side!*
> *The magic words we say with pride:*
> *Not just a spell, not just a curse,*
> *the secret works only in reverse!"*

I stared at the mixed-up letters on the ground. Instead of starting with an *S*, now the word started with an *R*.

"Hmm . . . the **secret** works only in reverse," I whispered to myself.

I quickly rearranged the sticks so that *Scorcher* was spelled BACKWARD.

I **JUMPED** up, ran toward the rock, and leaned my paw against it. Then I pronounced *Scorcher* backward: "**REHCROCS!**"

My paw sank into the rock!

Blue Rider's eyes opened wide in surprise, "You did it, mouse!" he exclaimed.

"What's all the **commotion**?" Harper complained, waking up.

"The mouse figured out the **MAGIC WORD**," Blue Rider explained. "Now let's start running. I don't know why, but for some reason the pixies hurl themselves against the rock at full **SPEED**. We better do the same, just in case."

So I started **running** at full speed. With all my might, I threw myself against the rock as I yelled the song:

"Beyond and yonder to the dark side!
The magic words we say with pride:
Not just a spell, not just a curse,

the secret works only in reverse!
Rehcrocs!"

But just before I hit the rock I had a horrifying thought: I was about to enter the **dark side**. Who would want to go there? Oh, why hadn't I thought this one through? Hadn't my aunt Sweetfur warned me about making $NAP decisions? Or was that my great-aunt Fussyfur? No, she was always telling me to *wash* my paws before I ate.

I was still thinking about my great-aunt when we reached the dark side. What was it like?

Let me just say, **dark** didn't even begin to cover it. . . .

TERROR CASTLE

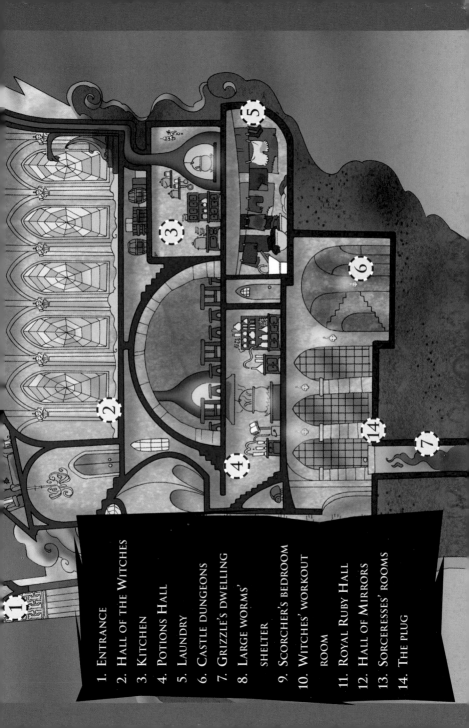

1. ENTRANCE
2. HALL OF THE WITCHES
3. KITCHEN
4. POTIONS HALL
5. LAUNDRY
6. CASTLE DUNGEONS
7. GRIZZLE'S DWELLING
8. LARGE WORMS'
   SHELTER
9. SCORCHER'S BEDROOM
10. WITCHES' WORKOUT
    ROOM
11. ROYAL RUBY HALL
12. HALL OF MIRRORS
13. SORCERESSES' ROOMS
14. THE PLUG

DON'T EAT THE INTRUDERS!

The castle on the other side of the rock was like nothing you've ever seen before. It was **horrifying**! And, as I stared up at the looming **MONSTROSITY** before us, I realized something equally horrifying. My feet weren't resting on the ground but on a layer of gray **clouds** that, like a drawbridge, were connected to the castle! Yep, there was no doubt about it. This was **TERROR CASTLE**, home to the evil Scorcher!

As it was illuminated by bolts of *LIGHTNING*, I realized that the castle was made entirely of spinning air! It created steep high walls, peaked by spires of **SNOW** and **ICE**. The towers were made of swirling hail, the roofs of black clouds,

and the windows of thin sheets of ice.

Oh, what a house of horrors!

It took me about two seconds before I turned as PALE as a slice of mozzarella.

"Um, so I guess the p-p-plan is to keep going into the c-castle. I mean, nobody wants to t-t-turn around and maybe come b-back tomorrow, right? Or maybe the n-next year?" I stammered.

Blue Rider POUNDED me on the back, trying to be encouraging. "We'll be fine. The witch has nothing on this hero. Who can compete with the best of the best?" he insisted.

I was still *wheezing* from his back slap when I noticed a whole squadron of witches heading right for us! They were riding enormouse fluorescent worms with green wings.

What a fright!

Suddenly, I found one directly in front of me. The worm had a **ROUND**, small head, beady little **EVIL** eyes, and tiny pointed teeth. A second later, I found out that those tiny pointed teeth were also razor-sharp, because one of them attacked me from behind, and with a bite that almost took off my tail!

HOLEY CHEESE!

I barely had time to catch my breath when what appeared to be the head witch arrived, *MASSIVE* and furious. Her flapping dress was decorated with black spiders and beetles. She **SCREAMED** out orders one after another, revealing huge decayed teeth every time she opened her mouth.

"Lightning Bolt Squad, advance! Archers, be ready to **ATTACK**! And remember: No one is to eAt the intruders. This large prey is intended for *her*!" she yelled.

LIGHTNING BOLT SQUAD

They shock with light and fry enemies in the night!

ARCHERS

They hurl arrows sharp and narrow!

FUMIGATORS

They'll make you choke with all their smoke!

FORK FORCE

They use forks to stab — they poke and jab!

IGNITERS

They throw fire wherever they desire!

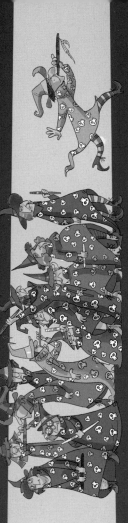

POISONERS

They use poison darts to pierce through hearts!

STINKERS

Their putrid stink will make you turn pink!

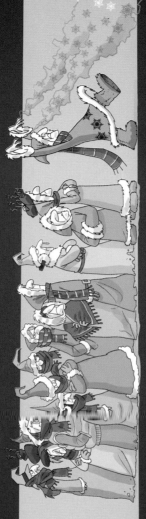

FREEZERS

Their icy freeze can make you stop mid-sneeze!

HAIL STORMERS

They shoot crushing hail that makes enemies wail!

INSULTERS

They insult everyone — they think it's fun!

SPIES

They are deadly spies in clever disguise!

SECRET REGIMENT

They're the scariest crew — no one knows what they do!

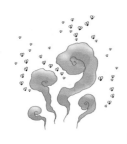

The band of witches **ATTACKED** us from every side.

The first to hit us were the Stinkers, who burped out disgusting smells!

I fainted instantly, but came to when I was shot in the snout with a **LIGHTNING BOLT** hurled by the Lightning Bolt Squad.

HOW SHOCKING!

When I smelled something burning, I looked around. *It's a strange time for a cookout,* I thought. Then I realized that the **burning** smell was coming from me! The lightning bolt had hit my whiskers!

Before I had time to even scream, the Archers began **launching** their arrows. The spray of arrows was so

thick I couldn't see a thing. But I did manage to catch Blue Rider **slicing** the arrows with his sword and even catching a few in his teeth! Pretty impressive.

As we were **DODGiNG** the Archers' arrows, the division known as the Insulters started offending us with every type of insult.

"Having a bad hair day, knight? Or is your barber *BLIND*?" they teased Blue Rider.

"Love the gold feathers, bird! Did you paint them on yourself?" they yelled at Clearfeathers.

Then they turned to me. I waited for the insults to fly, but instead they called out, "Get the **mouse**! He doesn't have a sword or a shield!"

Within minutes I was overwhelmed by the **ghastly** witches.

TERROR CASTLE

Even though I told him not to, Blue Rider lowered his sword and shouted, "I give up. Just leave the mouse alone!"

The witches surrounded us in an instant, cackling away. After they tied us up, they loaded us on top of the longest worm. Then they flew off in the direction of the castle. Eventually, we stopped in front of a large ice door on which something was written in the FANTASIAN ALPHABET. Can you translate it?* The answer is upside down on the next page.

*You can find the Fantasian alphabet on page 311.

Below it was another sign, on which was written:

ENTRY RESTRICTED TO WITCHES, SORCERESSES, MAGICIANS, CONJURERS, ENCHANTRESSES, HAGS, AND WIZARDS!

"Hmm. It doesn't say anything about mice or knights dressed in blue. Guess you better leave us here," I muttered to the witches. But no one listened.

Instead a young witch shouted at the door, "Open up! *It's me!*"

"Who's *me*?" a NASTY voice called.

"Me, the Head Witch of the Young Witches!" the witch called back

"I don't believe you. Whoever you are, **go away**!" the nasty voice answered.

The Head Witch shook her fist at the door

and **screeched** at the top of her lungs, *"I said, it's meeeeeeeeeee!"*

Unfazed, the voice behind the door retorted, "But how do I know it's **you**? I mean, give me some **proof**. What's my name?"

At this the Head Witch flew into a rage. "Listen, you subspecies of a toothless sorcerer, **GREEN**-faced maggot eater, wart-infested lizard puss, of course it's me! And you are **Garlicbreath**! They make you guard the door because the wind takes away your **stinky** breath and we smell it a little less!"

"Okay, okay, it's me, Garlicbreath. But you don't have to be so insulting. I have feelings, too, you know," the guard huffed.

Then she flung the door open and we entered the terrifying **TERROR CASTLE**.

IT WAS HER!

Tied to the back of the hideous winged **BIG WORM**, we flew through the halls with lightning speed, dodging walls and furniture and flying bats.

In the halls, a **frigid** wind was blowing so hard it made my whiskers quiver. Terrifying images passed before my eyes. There were witches everywhere, who seemed to be getting ready for a big **war**. Some were testing wands one by one to be sure they were capable of carrying out their **GHASTLY SPELLS**. Others were making concoctions and potions to use against enemies, and still others were practicing **acrobatic** flying moves on top of the big worms. To make way, the Head Witch shouted, "Shoo! Move! She's waiting for us!"

As soon as they heard her, the witches cheered, "Hooray!"

The Head Witch led us through an **immense** hall with a vaulted ceiling. The walls were covered with sheets of ice hanging at odd angles, giving the whole place a **warped** look, like the inside of a fun house.

Eventually, we reached a large circular room. It was lighted only by **creepy** candelabras in the shape of a skull. Bats of every shape and form hung from the ceiling. There were small ones, medium ones, fat ones, and gigantic ones. But all of them had frightening **RED** and **YELLOW** eyes that shone fiercely in the semi-darkness.

The Head Witch dropped onto the floor with a loud thud. She bowed and smiled, showing her few, **rotted** teeth.

"Here's the prey you were waiting for, O

Answer: There are 20 candles.

Ancient One! Do you want me to have them **BOILED**? Or would you prefer them **ROASTED**? How about ***stewed***?"

Then I saw her for the first time . . . it was her, Scorcher, the Ancient One with Eyes of **FIRE**!

Her face was *wrinkled* like a dried-up prune and she had a huge **wart** on her nose. She stared at me with her eyes half closed, but when she opened them, I realized they were as **RED** as a cherry on a slice of cheesecake at Pipsqueaks Café back in New Mouse City. Oh, how I wished I were home!

I was still thinking about home when the witch patted the gigantic scorpion by her side and **stretched** her lips into a wicked grin. "Now that you're my prisoners, the Ancient Gemstone Prophecy will never be fulfilled! All I need is the **Royal Sapphire** and I'll be invincible!" she said, cackling.

SCORCHER

S **corcher** is the Empress of the Witches, also called the Ancient One with Eyes of Fire. For many years, she's been ruling the dark forces in the immense lands of the Kingdom of Fantasy.

Her power extends over all creatures who have chosen wickedness, evil, and darkness, and over those who have been put under her spell. Her goal is to one day gain full control over the kingdom by capturing the Royal Sapphire, the treasured gemstone guarded by Azul.

It is said, however (even if no one dares to repeat it out loud), that long ago, Scorcher was not a witch, but a fairy. It is said that she was the most beautiful of all the fairies, the youngest and sweetest among the fairies, and that her eyes were as clear and blue as cornflowers in the spring. But don't mention her past, or she'll make you pay a deadly price!

TOASTED LICE AND CAMEL SPIT!

I was trying not to faint when I noticed a row of toads lined up near the witch's throne. Each one was wearing a costume. One was dressed like a knight in full armor, another like a court jester, and still another like a prince with a little crown. Was it Halloween already?

As I watched, Scorcher pointed to the nearest toad and commanded, "You! Bring me a salamander's tail smoothie, with some SLIMY fish scales, two ground-up slugs, a pinch of toasted lice, the spit of a camel, and some ant urine!"

Ouch!   Poor me!   Aaah!   Ugh!   Waah!   Ack . . .

When the toad didn't answer she shrieked, "**GOT IT?**"

The toad, confused, tried to recap what she had said, mumbling, "Ahem, okay, so you said a salamander's tail, two **toasted** slugs, a pinch of lice's spit, ahem, or maybe it was camel's urine and **ant's spit**, or was that —"

Before the toad could go on, the witch waved her wand at him.

Zap!

Instantly he became a little pile of **SMOKING** green ashes.

All the other toads in line trembled with fear.

Next, come forward!

Youch!

Help!

Ahem . . .

"Next, come forward!" she yelled.

"Get me some **DUNG BEETLE** stew with a splash of boar's hair, the spit of a camel, the sweat of a fly, a bee's saliva, a mosquito's stinger, and the tears of a scorpion!" Scorcher ordered.

The toad **HOPPED** away, panting.

"Yes, my lady!"

But after a couple of hops he turned around, unsure, and muttered, "Ahem, excuse me, **YOUR HORRENDOUS WICKEDNESS**. Did you say a fly's tears and a boar's saliva, or —"

She didn't answer — just made another stroke of her wand, and incinerated him.

ZAP!

Then the witch turned to me.

"What do we have here? A **mouse**? You have an intelligent face. Maybe you went to school. I really hope I don't have to **INCINERATE** you, too! Are you ready?"

Before I could answer, she screeched, "I want you to bring me a pair of lice skin slippers, a nightgown of braided **poison ivy**, and a robe of thorns. Then draw me a bath with salts from **POISONOUS** cyanide and bubbles of rotted swamp mud! And, oh, also get me a porcupine bristle toothbrush with **mummy's** dust toothpaste. Then prepare a **snack** for my scorpion companion: the larvae of a putrefied fly. GOT IT?"

She thought she had **OVERWHELMED** me, but as soon as she began to talk, I had pulled

...lice skin slippers...

How can you remember everything?

out Honor and taken note of everything. So, I calmly read back my **notes**.

"'Poison-ivy nightgown . . . thorny robe . . . poisonous cyanide . . . rotted mud . . . mummy's dust toothpaste' . . . Is that all, my lady?"

The red-eyed witch was so surprised, her jaw dropped.

All the other witches looked equally shocked.

I must say, I was feeling proud of myself until Scorcher said, "So, you can write? Good. Then you will become my new servant."

Greenish toad you will become . . .

Huh?

Then she raised her wand, placed it on my head, and chanted:

> *"Greenish toad you will become*
> *when my wand begins to hum.*
> *Obey me or pay the price:*
> *I'll turn your friend into head lice!"*

Before I could squeak, the witch's **WAND** began to hum. A strange feeling came over me, as if all my body's cells were being **MIXED UP**.

Then my paws shortened and my back curved forward. My precious whiskers disappeared along with my ears, and my fur turned into **SHINY GREEN** skin!

Oh no!

Help!

Croak!

RIBBIT! RIBBIT! RIBBIT!

I tried to scream, "Help! I'm a toad!" but all that came out was a deep "**Ribbit ribbit ribbit!**"

The witch beamed. "Perfect! This spell never fails me. Not that I ever mess up — I mean, I *am* the **BEST** — but this one came out extremely well! That **GREEN** is to die for!" she cackled.

Luckily, I still had Honor and Harper in my bag. I signaled for them to stay **QUIET**.

Meanwhile, the witches gave their leader a round of applause. "He looks *awesome*!

Ribbit!

Nobody toads them as well as you do, **Ancient One**!" they cheered.

Scorcher stared at me with her red eyes *BLAZING*. She screeched, "Now, listen up! From now on you will do everything I say. One **WRONG** move and your friends are toast. Got it?"

I quickly nodded and she laughed wickedly. Then she turned to Clearfeathers, "Your turn, birdy!" she screeched, waving her wand again. Instantly, a little IRON CHAIN clamped on to Clearfeather's foot. Scorcher handed the Head Witch the other end of the chain. "Your *prize* for bringing me the prisoners," she announced.

Finally, Scorcher turned to Blue Rider. She looked him up and down from head to foot, walking around him in a **slow** circle.

"Hmmm, you remind me of someone, but who?" she murmured, **TAPPING** her head.

The she shook her head and huffed, "Well, whatever! I don't have any time to waste. I'll put you in a *cage*, and then I'll figure out what to do with you!"

Turning to the witches, she announced, "And now I will whip up the **Flaming circle**!"

"Oh boy! The Flaming Circle! We love the **Flaming circle**!" the other witches cried.

I gulped. Something told me the Flaming Circle probably didn't involve the witches standing in a circle holding **neon** glow sticks.

The sound of a big black cauldron being dragged into the room interrupted my thoughts. The witches lit a ***crackling*** fire under it, then stood back as Scorcher approached it. She coughed, **cracked** her knuckles, and did **jumping jacks**. I guess even witches

needed to warm up before performing spells.

At last, she said, "Okay, let's see if I remember this spell correctly. . . ."

She began **SWIRLING** her wand and throwing peculiar ingredients into the pot one by one as she **sang** with a booming voice:

> *"Breath of dragon and bramble thorns,*
>   *poison ivy, rhinoceros horns,*
>   *add in rotten maggot slime*
> *then wave the wand one more time.*
> *Now Flaming Circle, light the ground*
> *and make a cage deadly and round!"*

Zap!

She burst into a ghoulish laughter, and traced a circle on the floor with her dripping wand. Three large witches threw Blue Rider into the center of the circle, and immediately a wall of **greenish flames** burst up around him. He tried to cross it, but the flames rose higher and higher, forming an impenetrable **barrier**.

Blue Rider looked like he would explode with anger. "You can't **stop** me! I'm the best!" he

Now what?

insisted. But after almost setting his boots on *fire*, he sat down. "Just resting," he muttered.

All the witches **clapped**. "More!" they cried.

Scorcher snorted, "No more. I don't have any other prisoners. But since we have a fire, we can **cook** dinner. Ladies, you're all invited!"

The shrieking witches dragged in tables and dishes. Once seated, they began **banging** the table with their mugs, cackling and chanting. "**WE ARE HUNGRY!** We are hungry!"

I was forced to cook and serve them the most *disgusting* food. I hopped from one witch to another, refilling bowls and pouring drinks. The whole time they played mean pranks on me, like **tripping** me and throwing **CABBAGE LEAVES** at my head.

DRAW MY BATH!

After a long, long time, the young witches were done stuffing their faces, and left the room. I was so exhausted I curled up in a ball by the **FIREPLACE** and fell asleep right away.

The next day at dawn, Scorcher summoned me and immediately began barking out orders.

"Toad, **COOK** me a soup of salamander, fish guts, and scorpions! Be sure they're fresh, tender, and succulent! *Wash* my underwear with mushroom **mold** and coyote dung! Draw my bath with SCALDING swamp mud, and

COOK SALAMANDER SOUP . . .   WASH WITH MUSHROOM MOLD . . .

perfume it with the breath of oysters! Bring me my stinky slippers, and after you **chew** on garlic, wash the windows with your spit! Be sure you spread the dust all over! And be careful of the spiderwebs! They're very old, and if you break any of them, you will mend them, one by one! And when you're finished *cleaning*, start writing my biography. Make it exciting, like me! Then after that, you'll SING to me! Don't give me that look, I know very well you have a harp and a pen hidden in your bag! Don't deny it! If you do, I'll use your skin to make a LAMPSHADE, the harp to make a coat hanger, and with the pen I'll make a toothpick. Got it?"

DRAW A BATH OF MUD . . .

BRING STINKY SLIPPERS . . .

Then she threw some **keys** at me, and hissed, "With these, you can open all the doors in the castle . . . except that **little red door**, which only opens with the little key I keep hanging on the wall in my room."

She shot me a menacing look.

"Beware, toad! Do not touch that key or go into the room with the red door. Not if you want to live! Now, quit **yakking** and get to work!" she demanded.

I wanted to point out that she was the one yakking, but figured now wasn't the time. As soon as the witch left, Honor peeked out of my bag and **grumbled**, "Sure, I'll write your biography. I'll call it *Scorcher: The Weirdo Witch with a Thousand Warts*!"

Next Harper jumped out and began to sing, "**Weirdo Witch!** Weirdo Witch!"

I didn't want to find out what the witch would do to us if she heard the harp's song, so I told Harper to keep **quiet**.

With a heavy heart, I began scrubbing the floors of the castle. If only I had that vial of Sapphire Water to use against the witches. But who knew where Clearfeathers had HIDDEN it?

At the end of the day, I found myself before the room the witch had FORBIDDEN me to enter. *Why doesn't Scorcher want me to go inside?* I thought.

There was only one way to find out. Get the key to that door!

Before I could change my mind, I HOPPED to Scorcher's bedroom.

Have you ever seen a witch's bedroom? Well, let me just tell you, this place was scarier than a cemetery at midnight! First of all, the bed had a creepy canopy made of BAT

WINGS, and it was covered with a blanket made entirely of what looked like **POISONOUS** leaves. On the bureau was a skull-shaped lamp with a shade made of GREEN SKIN. . . .

RANCID RAT HAIRS! Could it be . . . toad's skin?

"M-m-maybe we should come back another time," I mumbled, turning to leave.

But the pen stopped me. "Come on, we made it this far. Just hop up there, grab the key, and let's get out of here, Music Mouse! Or should I say, MUSIC TOAD?!"

It was then that I realized there are some advantages to being a toad. As a mouse, I would have needed a ladder to reach the key. Now all I had to do was take one giant hop.

Boing!

I snatched the key on the first try, and made my getaway.

WHO ARE YOU?

I hopped as **fast** as I could to the little red door and stuck the key in the lock. I found myself in a room made of **ice** with **RED** silk drapes on the windows. But what left me speechless was the enormouse ruby at the center of the room. It was the **Royal Ruby**, one of the precious gems from the Ancient Gemstone Prophecy. Here was Scorcher's beloved **treasure**!

I walked over to the ruby and tapped it with my paw — or, er, my webbed hand. Suddenly, it began to **quiver**, and I heard what sounded like a sad musical *sigh*.

Inside the ruby was a beautiful girl who was crying as she plucked leaves off of a **daisy** with never-ending petals.

The maiden wore a dark red velvet dress and

appeared to be **imprisoned** inside the treasured ruby! How bizarre!

I waved to attract her attention, and her eyes **widened** in shock. For a moment, she looked like she was about to faint. Then she pulled herself together and said in voice that sounded far away, "**Who are you?** I am Tenderheart."

"Ahem . . . my name is Stilton, *Geronimo Stilton* — that is, I'm Music Mouse. You see, I'm a rodent —"

The girl was surprised.

"Actually, you look like a **toad** to me," she said.

I coughed. "Well, yes. It's, um, sort of confusing. You see, I was **transformed** into a toad but I'm actually a mouse, and, er, in any case, I am here with Blue Rider to **SAVE** you," I babbled.

The girl's face brightened.

"Did you say **Blue Rider?**" she murmured.

I explained to Tenderheart that Blue Rider was stuck inside the **Flaming circle**, which was like a prison only with fire, and that the witch had **CHAINED UP** the bird who couldn't remember anything.

"It doesn't make total sense, but **DON'T WORRY**," I concluded. "I've got everything under control . . . well, sort of."

While I was talking, I noticed the key was ***rusty***, so I absentmindedly began polishing it with my dust cloth. Just then I heard the witch's steps echoing in the castle. Then I heard her voice.

"Drat — by a thousand toads' warts, I forgot my WAND. . . ." she fumed.

Cheese niblets! The witch was coming!

The sound of her **shuffling** feet came closer and closer, as did the stench of her vile slippers.

PEE-YOO!

I said good-bye to Tenderheart, promising I would return soon to rescue her, and **hopped** across the room and out the door.

By now, my heart was **POUNDING** up a storm under my slimy green skin, but I forced myself to keep going. When I reached Scorcher's room I stuck the key back on the wall *just in time.*

The witch barreled into her room like a **tornado**, screeching, "You've got a guilty look about you, mouse — I mean, toad. You didn't touch the key, did you?"

I quickly answered, "What **key**?"

"The key to the room with the red door. The one I told you **never** to enter if you value your life!" she cackled.

I pointed to the wall. "You mean that one?" I said, innocently.

With a **Leap** she grabbed the key, and when she saw it had been polished, she screeched, "Mouse — that is, toad — you'll pay dearly for this. *This key is clean!* Did you go into the room?"

I tried to defend myself.

"**NO!** I just cleaned it. I didn't go into the room. I didn't see the enormouse **RUBY** inside. . . ." I mumbled.

Ribbit!

Oh, why am I such a terrible **liar**?

The witch interrupted me, an evil look on her face. "**Aha!** If you didn't go into the room, how would you know that the **Royal Ruby** is there? That's it! You and your knight friend will be dinner for **Grizzle** tonight!" she cried.

Then she picked me up by the leg and dragged me away.

TENDERHEART

Scorcher gathered all of the witches together.

"Take the prisoners to the **DUNGEONS**!" she ordered. "I want to feed them to **Grizzle**!"

On hearing this, the witches exclaimed excitedly, "Oh boy, Grizzle!"

Scorcher handed me over to the Head Witch. Then she pointed her WAND at Blue Rider and turned the **Flaming circle** into a flaming chain so that he could be transported to the dungeon. I wanted to tell him about **Tenderheart**, but I didn't get a chance. Maybe it was a good thing. After all, what was the point of finding your lost love if you were about to be eaten by some sort of **MONSTER**?

The witches dragged us down a **spiral** staircase, which was carved out of ice. They stopped in front of a **snowy** door and then they turned the handle made of lightning bolts.

Whack!

The door flew open and we were **FLUNG** into a large, cold cellar. In the center of the cellar there seemed to be some sort of giant **PLUG**, like the kind you would find in a bathtub. How strange!

Ribbit!

The **WITCHES** gathered around the plug. Then the Head Witch commanded, "Okay, everyone, on the count of three, we're going to pull the plug."

She began counting out loud, "And a ONE, and a two, and a **three**!"

On the word three, there was a giant **POP**! After the plug was removed all that remained was a deep well. A strange cloud of gray SMOKE began coming out of the hole.

The smoke **swirled** faster and faster, like a tornado rising into the air. I wanted to turn away but I couldn't stop staring. What would emerge from the smoke? Another witch? A monster? A DANCING CLOWN? My old friend Stubbypaws? (I wonder what ever happened to him. We used to be so close. . .)

I was still thinking about Stubbypaws when I noticed a face emerging from the SMOKE.

Petrified with horror, I stared at it.

The face was enormouse, **MONSTROUS**, and feminine. Its eyes were closed, but its hair looked like thick, **wiggling** worms. . . .

Scorcher stepped forward, grinning.

"Oh, wicked Grizzle! Wakey, wakey!" she called.

She grabbed my arm and suspended me over the well.

"Grizzle, dear, look at what I brought! **A big, fat toad!**" she continued.

"Miss Grizzle, that's not true. I'm not a **toad**, I'm a mouse! And I'm not at all fat!" I insisted.

"Pipe down!" Scorcher grumbled.

But **Grizzle** didn't even bother opening her eyes. Disappointed, Scorcher threw me on the floor.

"Mouse — I mean, toad — you're not **big** enough, so she paid no attention to you! Better give her the knight. He's **bigger** than you!"

She beckoned the witches, who grabbed the greenish chain of *flames* tied around Blue

Ribbiiiit!

Rider's ankles and dragged him toward the pit.

Scorcher called out again, "OH, GRIZZLE, DARLING — DEAREST, LOOK WHAT I HAVE THIS TIME! YOU'LL LIKE THIS ONE!"

But again, nothing happened.

SCORCHER was silent for a long time, and then finally she threw her hands in the air. "Oh, all right, all right! Who am I kidding? I know what you're waiting for, Grizzle! I'll get you Tenderheart, and you can have these fools, too! Then I'll steal the Royal Sapphire, and the Kingdom of Fantasy will be mine, all mine! HA, HA, HA, HA! HA, HA, HA, HA! HA, HA, HAAAA!"

Scorcher waved her wand, and with a flash of red light, the Royal Ruby materialized.

At the center of the stone was the maiden **Tenderheart**. She looked around, confused, until she saw **Blue Rider**. He was so excited to see her, he almost got burned. The maiden smiled shyly and attempted to fix her **HAIR**.

Ah, **young love**!

But there was no time to rejoice. Scorcher had pulled out a giant **spiderweb**, and began chanting:

"Spiderweb,
make a net,
so the girl
I can get!"

She flung the web at the **RUBY** and it penetrated the stone.

Scorcher began pulling with all her might, **MOANING** and **groaning** the whole time. I guess she wasn't into exercising at the magical **WITCHES' GYM** we had passed on our way to the dungeon. (And I thought the gym back home was scary!) Finally, with one last tug, she **yanked** the giant web out of the stone — with Tenderheart trapped inside!

"Don't worry! **I'll save you!**" Blue Rider promised.

At this Scorcher cackled, "Um, in case you haven't noticed, knight, you have **flaming chains** around your ankles. And your friend the mouse is a **toad**. And your friend the bird doesn't even **REMEMBER** his own name."

BONK!

The other witches grabbed the maiden and dragged her toward the well. As she neared its edge, Tenderheart turned to Blue Rider. Batting her eyelashes, she said, "I'm sorry we had to meet under these circumstances, Blue. I mean, they wouldn't even let me take a SHOWER in all this time."

"Oh, but you look BEAUTIFUL," the knight assured her. "I'm sorry that I'm STUCK in these chains. I was hoping when I finally found you I could take you to dinner or a movie or something!"

Before the maiden could reply, the witches pulled her up to the edge of the well and called out, "Grizzle! Dinner is served!"

Right then, the monstrous creature woke

up. She opened her wide lips, revealing rows of **razor-sharp** teeth!

"Throw the girl in!" Scorcher shrieked.

Boiling blue cheese! Someone had to stop this madness or Tenderheart would be eaten alive!

Even though I was **trembling** with fear, I forced myself to **HOP** forward. "P-p-please, d-d-don't do it!" I croaked.

"P-p-please, d-d-don't do it!" Scorcher **mocked** me in a sing-song voice. "Tell me, who's going to stop me, mouse — I mean, toad? Certainly not you!"

Blue Rider wailed.

DEAR READER,

HAVE YOU EVER HAD A DAY WHERE

EVERYTHING GOES WRONG?

I HAVE. FOR EXAMPLE, ONE TIME MY ALARM CLOCK BROKE, SO I HAD TO SKIP BREAKFAST AND RUN TO THE OFFICE, BUT I FORGOT I WAS WEARING SLIPPERS, AND THEN IT STARTED RAINING. . . . ANYWAY, THIS WAS ONE OF THOSE DAYS! I DIDN'T KNOW HOW WE WOULD ESCAPE SCORCHER. BUT SOMETHING WAS ABOUT TO CHANGE. . . .

Okay, now, where was I? Oh, yes, the witches were about to throw Tenderheart into the well, when suddenly the Head Witch **tripped** on the hem of her dress. She ꝛolled on the floor, which broke the belt she wore around her waist, which released the **IRON CHAIN** that was holding Clearfeathers.

The bird was **free**! But before he could fly away, the Head Witch grabbed a broom and bonked him over the head.

BONK!

"Ouch!" Clearfeathers muttered, **flapping** his wings. A second later he opened his eyes wide. "Hey, I **REMEMBER** everything now!" he chirped. "You're Music Mouse! And you're Blue Rider! And I got hit on the head when we tried to cross that G°RGE and —"

I cut him off, whispering, "Do you remember where you hid the Vial of Sapphire Water?"

The bird lifted my cape, undid the seam with his beak, and held up the **Sapphire Water**! "Ta-da!" he sang.

So that's where the Sapphire Water was!

At last, everything began to make sense. The bird had sewn the vial into the hem of my cape while I was SLEEPING that night in the forest. That's why I had felt someone pulling at my clothes!

I was still thinking about the HiDDeN vial when Clearfeathers poured some of the blue liquid over my head.

"**Presto change-o!**" he chirped.

I immediately felt a very strong **tingling** sensation all over my body. First my face began to grow longer and longer, until I had a long snout and two ears on the top of my head.

Ribbit!

Ah!

Whiskers **Sprouted** around my nose, and brown fur shot out all over my body. Then I felt something pop out on my backside. . . It was my TAIL.

I became **TALLER** and **TALLER** and when I stretched, I realized I was finally back to my old self. My old, furry, squeaky, scampering rodent self!

"Yay! I'm me again! I mean, I'm not me as a toad — er, I'm me as a **mouse**!" I squeaked.

I was so happy to be myself again I didn't realize all of the witches were staring at me and **DROOLING**.

THROW IT!

Scorcher bellowed, "Get that mouse! *NOW!*"

The witches let go of Tenderheart, who *teetered* on the edge of the well. They took off after me, screaming, "Come here, mousey! *Nothing to be afraid of!* We won't lock you up! We just want to **EAT** you!"

Just when I thought I was about to be eaten by the witches, Clearfeathers threw me the vial of **Sapphire Water**, shouting, "Throw it on top of the witch!"

I caught it and heaved the contents onto Scorcher. She STARED at me in disbelief. Then she tried to grab me, but suddenly she began to grow SMALLER. A WISP of smoke rose from her head, enveloping her whole body. When the smoke cleared, the only thing left was a pile of ashes.

Suddenly, we found ourselves outside the castle — and it was now completely transformed! I was astonished. I slipped the Sapphire Water vial in my bag, even though we'd already used it.

Seeing the sunlight, the witches covered their faces with their knobby hands and long, POINTY nails and began wailing.

"Noooooooooooooooooooooo!"

But then the weirdest thing happened. The wailing turned into a choir of harmonious voices!

"Ooooooooooooooooooooooooooh!"

When the witches lowered their hands, their faces had changed. They were no longer witches. They had changed into FAIRIES!

Their hair flowed soft and long, and their skin was radiant. Their dark witch clothes had been replaced with brightly COLORED gowns.

The chains of fire that had held Blue Rider vanished, leaving only a slight trace of smoke

in their wake. As soon as the fire disappeared, the knight ran to Tenderheart. He scooped the maiden up into his arms, a huge smile lighting up his face.

"MY HERO!"

Tenderheart said, giggling.

"That's me!" Blue Rider agreed, **PUFFING** up his chest proudly.

How many
fairies don't have
wings?

Answer: 8 fairies don't have wings

Even the Head Witch had been transformed. She had become an elderly fairy with white hair and **BLUE** eyes. On her head she now wore a fairy hat with a very long, fluffy, candy-pink veil.

She came toward me, her long, **PiNK** gown rustling as she walked.

"Thank you for saving us! My name is Candace, but please call me CANDY — all my friends do!" she exclaimed, cheerily. "We were turned into witches under Scorcher's **spell**. But thanks to you, we are now faiRieS again!"

"You think that's bad. That's nothing," Clearfeathers ranted. "Try getting CLUNKED on the head and forgetting your own name, and then being chained up to a witch and not knowing whether you're going to live or die!"

I put my paw up and stopped him. "Um, CLEARFEATHERS, why don't we let

Candy tell us her story now?" I suggested. And so the fairy began.

"A long time ago, when Scorcher was actually the most beautiful, the sweetest, and the **HaPPiest** of fairies, I was her former governess, and her advisor. Eventually, she left for her husband's castle, where she lived **HAPPILY** for a year. Then, one day, no one knows why, she suddenly returned here — but she had turned into a witch! She threw a

spell on us and her castle." Candy paused, sighing. "We spent many years unwillingly as witches!"

TWO HEARTS

We all shook our heads in sympathy listening to Candy's sad story.

"I guess we all have sad stories to tell," Tenderheart added. "I've been TRAPPED in that gemstone for so long, I don't even know what year it is, or what's the latest style. I mean, are PUFFY sleeves still in? And what about patent leather shoes? Does anyone wear **patent leather** anymore?" she asked, staring at her feet.

"Don't worry, you'll always be my style," Blue Rider assured the maiden, causing her to giggle. Then the two gazed at each other, grinning from ear to ear.

Clearfeathers rolled his eyes. "Okay, lovebirds, enough of this mushy stuff. You've still got a mission to complete," he remarked.

Candy looked at the knight and the maiden in amazement. "Oh my goodness. You are the **TWO HEARTS** from the Ancient Gemstone Prophecy*!" she exclaimed. "Now the hardest part of your mission will start. You must unite the two treasured gemstones: the **Royal Ruby** and the **Royal Sapphire**."

"Yes," I said, "But how are we ever going to **transport** the enormouse ruby to Shining Moon Mountain?"

*You can find the prophecy on page 38.

I'm going!

"I can't carry the **Royal Ruby**. But you'll need a **GUIDE**, so I've decided I'm coming with you, Music Mouse!" Clearfeathers announced.

Honor jumped up next, **splattering** ink. "Well, if the bird goes, I go. You'll need someone to _write_ down all of your adventures, and that's my specialty! I'll write the TRUTH,

I'm going

the whole truth, and nothing but the truth!" she proclaimed.

I'm going!

At this, Harper plucked a chord. "And what about me?" she sang. "If the pen goes, I go! I'll cheer everyone up with my songs — that's my specialty! Ah, my voice is such a wonderful **GIFT**!"

"It's a **GIFT**, all right," Honor snickered.

"What's that supposed to mean?" Harper retorted.

Before long, the two were arguing.

Meanwhile, Candy was studying the **Royal Ruby**.

"Hmm . . . there's got to be a way to carry it," she said, thoughtfully.

Then she picked up her wand. "Let's see. I could change a **PUMPKIN** into a coach. . . . Nah, too ordinary! A turnip into a **HoRSe**? No, too weak! An apple into an *apple pie*? Not much help, but I would love a slice! I skipped lunch and I'm starving," she babbled.

I was beginning to think we'd **NEVER** figure out how to lift the huge ruby when Candy suddenly

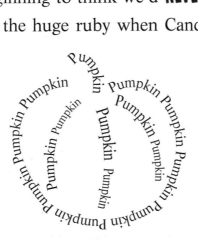

declared, "I've got it! What you need is a silver net pulled by **gigantic** swans."

She waved her magic wand in the direction of a group of seven **WHITE SWANS** swimming in the castle's moat and said:

"Feathered swans, so white and pure,
grow until you grow no more!"

Immediately, the swans started GROWING in front of our eyes!

Next, the fairy pulled three blades of grass from the ground and, pointing at them with her magic wand, said:

"*Blades of grass, green and long,*
weave a net that's super strong!"

The three strands of grass began to grow, **braiding** and weaving themselves as they got longer, until they formed a huge silver net that WRAPPED tightly around the ruby and then tied itself around the body of the swans.

Finally, Candy clapped her hands and all the young fairies began flitting about on their

Zap!

transparent *wings*, helping us get ready for our journey.

One whipped up a delicious-smelling batch of what looked like fairy scones. Another mended a hole in my shirt. Another *brushed* Blue Rider's horse, Snowy, and another drew us a detailed map of the area.

When everything was ready, Blue Rider and Tenderheart JUMPED on the horse, and the swans opened their wings, ready to take flight.

Harper sang a **farewell song** and all the fairies wished us well and waved good-bye.

There was only one problem. I needed a ride!

Just then Candy noticed my dilemma, and chuckled, "Oh, *silly me*, how could I forget you, Music Mouse! You need a mode of transportation. Now, let's see, the swans are all taken, so you'll have to make do with **Quackenbeak**."

The fairy pointed to a fat duckling sitting by a bush.

"Quackenbeak, please come here!" she called.

"Quack!" said the duck, **WADDLING** over.

Candy waved her wand at him and said:

"Quacking duckling, do not hide,
for you will be the mouse's ride!"

The duckling began to grow **bigger** and **bigger**. When he stopped, I climbed on his back and we walked — or, rather, **WADDLED** — toward Shining Moon Mountain.

Quackenbeak

Quackenbeak was Scorcher's favorite duckling when she was still a fairy, and even when she became the most wicked of witches, she wanted him near her . . . so she transformed him into a giant scorpion!

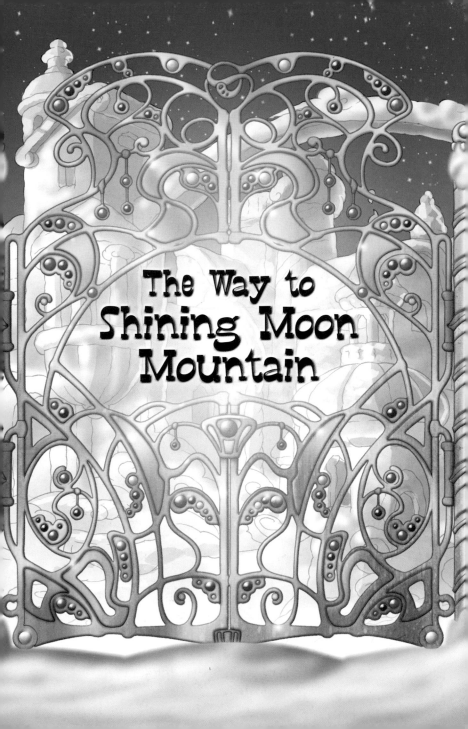

The Way to
Shining Moon
Mountain

THE WAY TO SHINING MOON MOUNTAIN

1. DRAGON'S DEN
2. HOT PEPPER WOODS
3. TERROR CASTLE
4. FOREST OF THE DROOLING TROLLS
5. THE FLOWER FAIRIES' MEADOW
6. GOBLIN POINT, ROYAL PALACE OF THE GOBLINS OF FLOWERS
7. SHINING MOON MOUNTAIN
8. SHRIEK PEAK
9. SAPPHIRE CITY, THE CITY AMONG THE CLOUDS
10. AZUL'S PALACE

How Gross!

The swans took off into the air carrying the ruby as Quackenbeak **WADDLED** after them, his humongous webbed feet slapping the ground. **SLAP! SLAP!**

It was a beautiful day. The sky was **blue**, the sun was **SHINING**, and a gentle breeze caressed my fur. Ah, my precious fur! I was so happy to have all of my old mouse parts back again. I must admit, that green toad skin and all that croaking kind of got on my nerves.

Anyway, where was I? Oh, yes, I was enjoying the gorgeous day. *Maybe the last part of my journey will be calm and relaxing,* I thought. *Little did I know how wrong I was!*

Soon everyone began quarreling. Harper decided to make up a *love song* for Blue Rider and Tenderheart and was singing at the top of her lungs, "**She wears red and he wears blue! They're in love, *doo doo doo doo!***"

"Are you kidding? That's the **worst** song ever!" Honor scoffed.

"Oh, like you could do any better?" the harp shot back.

"Quiet! I'm trying to **concentrate** on where we're going!" Clearfeathers screamed.

Meanwhile, Quackenbeak's waddling from side to side was making me nauseated. I held on, feeling more **sick** with every step. It didn't

Slap! Slap! Slap!

help that Quackenbeak never stopped quacking.

"QUACK! QUACK! QUACK!" he quacked as he waddled along. "Look at all the pretty flowers. Hey, I wonder if there's a pond around here. I miss my pond. It's so COOL and calm and relaxing. Plus, it's full of good things to eat, like tiny fish eggs, SNAILS, algae, and all sorts of seeds and berries. You think we might find a POND along the way? I could go for a quick dip. . . ."

I wanted to remind the duck that we were on a mission, but I couldn't get a word in!

YIKES . . . what a terrible trip!

I couldn't wait until it was over.

Finally, on the evening of the seventh day, I saw a chain of very high MOUNTAINS under a shining moon.

"That's it! I, your professional guide bird,

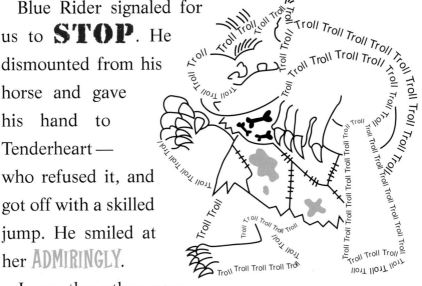

give you **Shining Moon Mountain!**"
Clearfeathers announced with a dramatic wave.

Blue Rider signaled for us to **STOP**. He dismounted from his horse and gave his hand to Tenderheart — who refused it, and got off with a skilled jump. He smiled at her ADMIRINGLY.

I, on the other paw, clambered off Quackenbeak while he was still quacking away about ponds and fish and berries and **BLAH, BLAH, BLAH.**

Suddenly, in the middle of all the quacking, we heard a loud whistle.

I looked around and noticed that the trunks of the trees were dripping with STINKY, **gelatinous** lumps.

Suddenly, a hundred ugly, mean faces looked out from the branches and began pelting us with the same **disgusting** guck I had seen falling from the trees.

"Look out! They're Spitting Trolls. They're throwing **goop** at us — it's their horrible secret weapon!" Clearfeathers explained.

How GROSS and rude!

SECRET WEAPON No. 1
GOOP

Before attacking their victims, the Spitting Trolls chew the fruit of the Gum Tree and fill their mouths with a sticky, green, foul-smelling gelatin called goop. They then take this gummy goop and form balls, which they fling at their victims ... who have a hard time getting it off!

GO WITH
THE GLOP

"Hey, professional guide bird, you think you could have told us earlier about the fearsome **Spitting Trolls** living here?" Blue Rider complained.

"I thought it wouldn't be a problem for you, **HERO**. After all, you are the best of the best, right?" Clearfeathers replied with a wink.

Tenderheart grabbed a branch and began **FIGHTING** off the trolls. "You two want to stop **yakking** and help me out here?" she said.

Embarrassed, the knight ran to her side while the bird started pecking the trolls with his beak.

Peck! Peck! Peck!

"Youch!" yelped the trolls, beginning to retreat. Just when we thought the battle was over, a big, fat **troll** with an enormouse nose, a hairy chin, and long fingernails growled, "We can't take them down with the **goop**. Let's use the second secret weapon. Go with the **glop**!"

Then she began to sneeze repeatedly. And the rest of the trolls did the same. The results were so *disgusting*, I'd probably get sick describing it. Let's just say, when I was done with this adventure, I planned on taking the longest **BATH** of my life!

SECRET WEAPON No. 2

GLOP

The second secret weapon of the Spitting Trolls is glop. It's a nonstop sneeze that is discharged at great speed. Here we see a microscopic image of it. The germs and bacteria of the glop wear helmets because they're ejected at supersonic speed!

Glop under the microscope

As the trolls began to sneeze **glop** at us, we took shelter behind a rock. But after a while Blue Rider decided enough was enough. He stood up, **drew** his sword, and went on the attack. Talk about taking one for the team!

When the trolls saw they weren't able to **DEFEAT** us by using their unrelenting sneezes, a little troll screeched, "Forget the goop! Forget the glop! Let's go with the **gagger**!"

Then he emitted something from his mouth that felt like a **HURRICANE**.

BUUUUUUUURRRRP!

All the flowers nearby **WITHERED**, and

leaves rained down.

The gagger almost **BLEW** us away! Blue Rider grabbed hold of a tree, Tenderheart held on to him, I held on to her, and Clearfeathers held on to my hood. Is this how it would all end? Brought down by a BURP?

SECRET WEAPON No. 3
THE GAGGER

The Spitting Trolls' last secret weapon is the gagger. When unleashed, it's like a hurricane or tornado. Flowers wither, leaves fall off the trees, and everything is blown away in a vortex of wind.

UGH, ROSES!

Just when it seemed like all was lost, something incredible happened.

No, the trolls didn't start *singing* and **dancing** a jig. They just stopped burping, and instead they started sniffing. . . .

Then they began to retreat!

"**BLAH!** What's that horrible perfume?" they groaned.

They all sniffed the air with disgusted frowns.

"**Yuck!** It almost smells like . . . the perfume of flowers!"

Just then we noticed thousands of **tiny** winged creatures emerging from the flowering meadow before us. They were dressed in **BRIGHTLY COLORED** clothes.

One creature who seemed to be their leader shouted, "**Attack! Use the perfume!**"

Before the trolls could think of **plugging** their noses (in case you didn't know, trolls are not the brightest bulbs in the box!), the little fairies went on the attack. By using miniature catapults, they shot a rain of little balls of soft, **rose-scented** wax toward the trolls. The wax stuck all over their **stinky** bodies.

Other fairies sprayed streams of perfume through the air, adding the scents of **LAVENDER** and wild roses.

"This is great!" Honor shouted, popping out of my pouch to watch the action. "Don't worry, mouse, I'm taking notes on everything! I've got the spitting, the sneezing, the burping, and now the perfume." She paused, sniffing the air. "Mmm . . . I wonder if the fairies would mind bottling some of that rose scent for me. It's so pretty and *sweet*."

"I kind of like the **LAVENDER** scent," Harper chimed in. "Or is that honeysuckle?"

While the two chatted away, the rest of us watched the fairies and the trolls.

What an incredible battle of smells!

Finally, the trolls couldn't take all of the **pretty smells** anymore, and took off shrieking back into the forest.

"Ugh, roses are the worst!"

"No way, **LAVENDER** is disgusting!"

"I can't even smell my own **stink** anymore!"

As soon as they were far enough, the Flower Fairies began **cheering**. "We **won**!"

I knelt down, so I could be at their height, and thanked them. Right then two fairies **flitted** over on their **green** wings and landed on my snout.

"My name is Poplar and this is my wife, Primrose. We're the guardians of **FAIRY**

MEADOWS. And you must be Music Mouse, Blue Rider, and Tenderheart. We heard you were coming our way. We're so glad we could help you out, and —"

But before he could continue, the most **embarrassing** thing happened. The weight of the fairies standing on my snout made it **itch**, which led to a *tickly* sensation, which led to a . . . sneeze!

My sneeze **BLEW** all the fairies out into the meadow.

"Uh, thanks again!" I called as they waved good-bye.

HOW MORTIFYING!

Flit!

My name is Poplar!

Let's Move!

After the fairies left, we sat down to discuss the best way to climb up the treacherously **STEEP** Shining Moon Mountain.

Worried, I squeaked, "How are we ever going to Climb all the way to the top? We don't have hiking boots, or ropes, or helmets, or any other kind of SAFETY gear."

"That's not the real problem, mouse. The real problem is, how are we going to accomplish all that the *prophecy* asks? I mean, we have the **RUBY** and we've reunited the two **HEARTS**. But in order for the GEMSTONES to become one, we have to reunite a mother with her son and a husband to his wife," Blue Rider said.

Clearfeathers flew to the **TALLEST** tree and reported back, "Yep, not seeing any mothers or sons or husbands or wives or brothers or —"

Tenderheart **jumped** to her feet and interrupted the bird. "Well, there's only one way to make this prophecy happen, and that's to get going. No sense sitting around. Let's move!" she declared.

Blue Rider grinned at the maiden. "Isn't she great?" he said, staring at her lovingly.

"Here we go with the **mushy stuff** again," grumbled Clearfeathers.

The knight nodded to the swans, who took flight with the net holding the **Royal Ruby**. Then he turned to his horse.

"I think it would be best if you and **Quackenbeak** go back to Candy's castle. The road will become too **STEEP** for you, and I don't want you to hurt your precious horsey hooves. Okay, my Snowy-bowy? Okay, Quackywacky?"

"No problem," Quackenbeak told the knight. "But if you don't mind, can you not call me Quacky-wacky?"

Before we left, Tenderheart decided she needed a costume change. She borrowed Blue Rider's sword and **SNIPPED** the bottom of her long dress off.

"There, finally I can move more freely!" she said, kicking her legs that were now unburdened of the long, **HEAVY** material.

She *wound* her long blonde hair around her head with a piece of the dress she had cut.

Much better!

"Ah, much better. **I'M READY!**" she announced.

Blue Rider looked at her in amazement. "What a great idea!" he marveled.

"Yep, great, great, **great**!" Clearfeathers squawked. "Let's get this show on the road!"

So we continued on our long trek toward **Shining Moon Mountain**.

We walked the entire night until we reached the mountain. The following morning, we began the very long climb up the STEEP SLOPES. It was tough going. My paws **slid** painfully on the frozen rocks. The frigid **wind** swept mercilessly along the frozen ridge we were traveling on, blowing into every opening of our clothes. Even the swans were in **TROUBLE** as the wind dangerously rocked the silver net that held the **RUBY**.

After walking for hours and hours,

I'm ready!

disaster struck. The net suddenly BROKE with a loud **snap**! The ruby fell — and almost squished me!

I'd say my life *FLASHED* before my eyes, but it was snowing so badly I couldn't see a thing! "**FROZEN FURBALLS!**" I shrieked.

We were forced to **PULL** the ruby up the icy, treacherous mountain.

Oh, what I wouldn't have given to be sitting in my favorite pawchair at home with a cup of *hot cheese*!

Just when I thought things couldn't get any worse, Harper decided to sing an earsplitting song:

"I can't take it!
We'll never make it!"

"Shhhhh! You don't want to cause an **avalanche**," Blue Rider cautioned. But just as he uttered his last word we heard a *tremendous* roar. . . .

A second later, we were hit by an avalanche of **snow** that carried us down a steep slope.

WELCOME TO SAPPHIRE CITY!

"Quick, climb on!" Blue Rider shouted.

He and Tenderheart jumped onto the ruby as if it were a **surfboard**. I grabbed on the back, and we began **spiraling** wildly as we went down . . . down . . . down . . . down. . . .

The good news is, we eventually came to a stop at the bottom of the mountain. The bad news is, we stopped by crashing

Argh!

into an enormouse pile of snow and ice. **YOUCH!**

But after I painstakingly dug myself out of the snow, I saw before us a GOLDEN GATE studded with **pearls**. Two warriors garbed in snow-white garments guarded the gate with stern expressions.

I cleaned my glasses to make sure I wasn't **seeing** things. Nope, the guards were still there. And when they spotted us, they threw open the mysterious gate, saying, "Welcome to **Sapphire City**, home of Azul, the Ancient One with Eyes of Sapphire."

I walked through the gate and my jaw hit the ground. We were in some sort of HIDDEN valley — a fantastic world made of **SOFT**, frothy clouds. I felt like I was in whipped-cream heaven!

Dragging the **heavy** ruby, we walked through the immense city. It really was one of the most **SPECTACULAR** places I'd ever seen! Just imagine

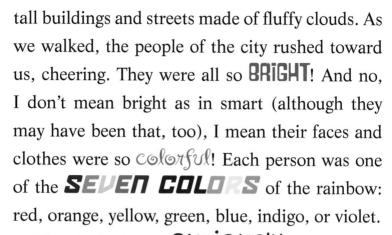
tall buildings and streets made of fluffy clouds. As we walked, the people of the city rushed toward us, cheering. They were all so **BRiGHT**! And no, I don't mean bright as in smart (although they may have been that, too), I mean their faces and clothes were so *colorful*! Each person was one of the **SEVEN COLORS** of the rainbow: red, orange, yellow, green, blue, indigo, or violet.

They looked at us **curiously** and pointed.

"It's them!"

"Could it be?"

"Yes, the heroes from the prophecy. Look, they have the **Ruby** here!"

Feeling a little **embarrassed**, I mumbled, "Ahem, actually, we weren't really that successful. You see, we have the **Ruby**, but we weren't able to reunite two spouses, and we couldn't find the mother and the son, and —"

Before I could finish, a maiden came forward.

"Don't worry. **AZUL**, the Ancient One with Eyes of Sapphire, will take care of the **IMPOSSIBLE**. Please, follow me," she said in a friendly voice.

We followed her along an avenue of soft clouds. The road was flanked by a MULTICOLORED crowd that cheered as we passed by. We crossed the entire city, until the maiden stopped before the simplest, most *modest* building of them all.

Surprised, I asked, "Where's Azul's **palace**?"

"Here, before you!" answered the maiden, pointing to a **little blue** door, on which a sign was written in the Fantasian alphabet.

Can you translate it?*

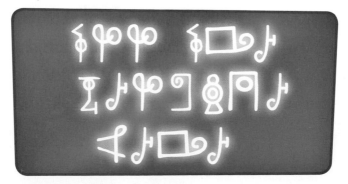

You can find the Fantasian alphabet on page 311.

It said, "*All are welcome here!*" As I read the sign, seven humongous guards, dressed in the seven colors of the **rainbow**, thundered toward us.

"Azul sent us. We need to take the **Royal Ruby** to the Transformation Hall," one of the guards said.

The guards lifted the ruby effortlessly and took it into a building right next to Azul's palace.

We followed them through the little **BLUE**

door, which opened up into a bare hallway. The place was **crowded** with people of all ages. Everyone seemed to be waiting for something.

Were they waiting to buy **concert** tickets? Was the circus in town?

Our guide explained. "Every day **AZUL** receives his subjects. He listens to everyone and gives them advice and help. As long as someone needs him, his door is always open."

What a **NICE** man! We joined the crowd and waited our turn. Besides solving the prophecy, I wondered if I could ask Azul some other questions. Like how to make grilled cheese without *BURNING* the bread, or how to keep my whiskers from *poking* me in the eye in a windstorm . . .

AZUL, THE ANCIENT ONE WITH EYES OF SAPPHIRE

While we waited and waited, Blue Rider excused himself for some fresh air. But when we were finally called in to meet Azul, Blue Rider had still not returned. **HOW STRANGE!** Did he get lost finding fresh air in a city built of clouds?

But there was no time to worry about the knight. **AZUL** was ready for us. He was seated in a simple carved WOODEN chair, wore a white cloak and had eyes as BLUE as sapphires. When he saw us, he smiled and welcomed us.

"Hello, O Kingly One — or, er, Your Sapphireness . . ." I stammered, BOWING so deeply I accidentally banged my snout on my knee.

"Call me **AZUL**," the leader said,

laughing. "And you are Music Mouse. But don't worry, I won't reveal your other names yet, because that is your wish."

Just then Clearfeathers hissed in my ear, "He can read what you're THINKING!"

Azul went on. "Hmm, I see that you are sad about not having completed your mission. But you should not be worried. I also see that you have good intentions and a good heart and also, well, you can't wait to have a mozzarella milk shake when you get home."

I smiled sheepishly. How embarrassing!

Finally, Azul closed his eyes and, turning serious, said, "The moment has come. Let us go to the HALL OF TRANSFORMATIONS!"

He got up and we followed behind his seven rainbow-colored guards. We walked along a NARROW corridor until we came to an ENORMOUSE room.

At its center, I saw two stones on the floor: the **RoyaL Ruby** and the **Royal Sapphire** the prophecy had spoken of!

Astonished, I noticed the two stones had the same shape and size.

I stared at the Royal Sapphire gleaming in the light next to the Royal Ruby. They looked so perfect together, like two gems cut from one **giant** stone. Too bad the prophecy would never come true. If only we had found those two spouses and that mother and son. I wondered where they could be. Could we have passed them along the way?

I was still thinking about the prophecy when a **DaZZLiNG** figure came walking toward us. It was a knight in a shining Silver suit of armor. At his side hung a very **SHARP**, familiar-looking sword. I tried to get a better look, but all of the people of the city had rushed forward,

Here is the Royal Sapphire!

whispering, "I can't believe it. . . . It's him!"

"Azul's son has come back!"

"It's definitely him! The **Silver Knight**, the protector of the poor, the defender of the defenseless, the hero of the helpless and the hopeless, the best of the best!"

The BEST OF THE BEST? I scratched my head. Where had I heard that before?

The knight came toward me and I *extended* my paw. "Um, it's an honor to meet you, I am the mouse — er, the Music Mouse," I babbled.

The silver knight laughed a very familiar laugh. "I know you well, Music Mouse. Don't you know who I am?" he asked.

Maybe it was all the *colorful* people of Sapphire City that were distracting me, but for whatever reason my brain just didn't seem to be functioning. Who was this **MASKED** man?

"Uh, you're the **Silver Knight**, the

Poor Protector, the Helpless Helper?" I guessed.

The knight burst out laughing again and **RAISED** his helmet. "You forgot 'best of the best'! Not to mention **DARING**, courageous, and charming!" he added.

Only then did I recognize him. Of course, it was Blue Rider!

"I can't believe you're Azul's son!" I squeaked.

Blue Rider GRINNED. Then, holding Tenderheart's hand in his, he turned to his father.

Don't you know who I am?

Ummm . . .

DAWN IS NEARING!

Blue Rider announced, "Father, this is Tenderheart, the maiden I *love*. And this rodent is my **FRIEND**."

Azul bowed his head.

"Of course, my son. I already know who they are. I can read inside *hearts*, you know," he said calmly.

Then he put his arm around Tenderheart. "Welcome, maiden," he said, smiling. "Anyone who is dear to my son is dear to me."

Without warning, the harp began to **cough** loudly, trying to attract the King's attention. "Oh, Your Highest Highness, Noble Sapphire King, Ancient Leader of the COLORFUL people," she sang. "Don't forget us! We, too, are friends of your son."

Mortified, everyone in the room fell silent. But Azul grinned warmly.

"I would never forget you, Harper, or you, **HONOR**, or you, CLEARFEATHERS. You have all been good friends to my son!" he proclaimed.

He nodded and the court's astronomer beat a gong, whose sound reverberated throughout the great hall. . . .

The astronomer announced, "Dawn is nearing! The Morning *STAR* is about to rise. . . ."

I turned toward Azul.

"Ancient One, forgive us," I squeaked sadly. "We were not able to bring our mission to completion. We didn't *unite* all the couples we were supposed to — not the two spouses, nor the mother with her son."

At this the King shook his head and said, "**Have faith!** Not everything is what it seems. . . . "

He turned to the **ASTRONOMER**. "Proceed!"

The astronomer cleared his throat. "Well, if the heroes had completed the mission, the **light** from the **MORNING STAR** would have hit the Royal Ruby and the Royal Sapphire, uniting them and bringing **PEACE**. But there are only two hours left until dawn, so I think, well . . . basically, we're **doomed**."

Everyone fell silent and gave us sad looks.

I gnawed on my whiskers, feeling like a total failure. How did this happen? I **always** completed my missions in the Kingdom of Fantasy. Would I ever be invited back again?

Only Azul seemed **CALM**.

"Have faith. Not everything is what it seems." he repeated.

I had no idea what Azul meant, but just being in his presence made me feel better. He was so PEACEFUL.

Then he said, "Why don't we all relax? It's such a **BEAUTIFUL** night here in Sapphire City. Can you play something cheerful, Harper?"

And so the harp (who was dying to show off her musical talent) began singing a paw-tapping song:

"It's a gemstone-colored night in the city of light!
The clouds make everyone feel all right.
Come on, tap your feet to my musical beat
and wish for a world that is kind and sweet!"

Singing and dancing, we awaited the arrival of dawn.

No Fair!

The astronomer checked an enormouse **hourglass** and announced, "It's four fifteen. Everyone please line up. The **MORNING STAR** is about to rise!"

I put my bag on the floor. But as I walked to the other side of the room, I had the **STRANGEST** sensation. It felt as if something **wicked** was staring at me from the corner near my bag. I whirled around, but I only saw a shadow that DISAPPEARED in the blink of an eye. **WEIRD!**

I turned back to see the astronomer, who was adjusting the big gemstone lens that would REFLECT the rays of the Morning Star.

I whirled around again and this time I distinctly saw a **dark shadow**...

"Get ready!" the astronomer called.

And then the strangest thing happened. A CROAKING voice filled the room, snarling, "I'm ready!"

A cloud of smoke came out of my bag and slithered along the floor until it came to Azul.

The cloud of smoke began to **grow** and grow and **GROW** . . . until it grew as tall as Azul. But he remained calm and serene.

The **dark cloud** was becoming more and more defined. First, long robes began to appear, then a pointy hat, then a big, **beaked** nose with a wart on it. . . .

Suddenly it hit me. It was **SCORCHER**! We all shrank back in fear as she turned to Azul.

"Okay, Mr. Blue Eyes, it's come down to this. I, Scorcher, guardian of the Royal Ruby and

One, two, three . . .

wickedest witch around, **challenge** you!
Whoever wins will have *power* over the entire
Kingdom of Fantasy. Agreed?"

Azul agreed with a simple nod.

"We will each take ten paces, then we'll turn
around, and the **challenge** will begin!" the
witch cackled.

Without waiting for an answer, the witch turned
and walked away, counting her steps.

"One, two, three . . ."

Azul walked in the opposite direction. The witch continued counting,

"Four, five, six, seven, eight, nine . . ."

We all held our breath, waiting for the battle to begin. Scorcher had a **SMUG** look on her face, but Azul looked **STRONG** and determined. Who would win? It was all up in the air now. Well, technically it was up in the clouds, but that's beside the point. . . .

Then, before the witch said "ten," she whirled around and pointed her wand at Azul. A bolt of **fiery** red light shot out.

"Watch ouuuuuut!" we warned the king.

Take that!

But Azul, without bothering to turn, had already JUMPED aside. The bolt of light missed him and crashed against the throne, incinerating it.

"No fair!" Blue Rider shouted. "You never said ten!"

Scorcher snickered wickedly.

"Who says witches fight fairly?" she cackled.

The witch waved her magic wand again, chanting:

Stop the witch's evil spell!

"Balls of fire, hit your mark!
Turn Azul forever dark!"

Globes of BURNING fire flew through the air, but Azul quickly held his hands out in front of him and chanted:

"Shield of light, keep me well
and stop the witch's evil spell!"

A **SHIELD** of light formed around him, and the fiery globes BOUNCED off of it. This sent Scorcher into a tantrum.

Next, the witch conjured up a spell using the ferocious north wind. She opened her arms **WIDE** and the huge windows around the room were flung open with a loud **thud** as if pulled by invisible hands. Then a twister of *cold wind* with the strength of a hurricane rushed toward Azul with lightning speed.

Now, let me just say, if a *cyclone* of wind were headed toward me, I'd be running as fast as my paws could carry me. Not Azul: He just looked straight at the wind and sent it *racing* back toward Scorcher.

Needless to say, she was furious.

She drew a spiral in the air, forming another *cyclone*. This one was filled with poisonous scorpions, hissing snakes, bats with eyes of fire, and hairy-legged spiders!

What a nightmare!

Azul drew a spiral in reverse, and the twister began sucking all those horrific creatures inside itself. He thundered:

> *"Evil never conquers good!*
> *Give up, witch, as you should!"*

WELCOME BACK!

Unfortunately, the last spell greatly weakened Azul. He became *paler* and paler. Scorcher noticed it, and increased the strength of her **attacks**.

"There's one thing that could save Azul," suggested Tenderheart. "**Sapphire Water** would counteract the witch's **evil**. Too bad we don't have any."

I groaned. Just my luck — I had already used all the **Sapphire Water** I had been given!

I took the vial out of my pocket and showed it to the

Give up, witch!

maiden. And then I realized that there was one last **tiny drop** of Sapphire Water left!

I **threw** the vial to Azul, shouting, "Try this!"

He grabbed the VIAL and poured out the last drop onto his hand. The liquid **dribbled** out and multiplied as he repeated:

> *"Evil never conquers good!*
> *Give up, witch, as you should!"*

The drops bonded, forming a waterfall that **flooded** the great hall. The witch tried to run away, but the waves lapped at her dress and she began to change.

Nooooo!

Her shoes and dress transformed into elegant blue. She grew taller and her face became sweeter.

Her hair was the last to change. It went from being rough and SNARLED to being smooth and braided with pearls. When the witch raised her head, her EYES looked like they belonged to an entirely new person! It was a miracle makeover!

"Welcome back, my dear!" said Azul, grinning. Talk about STRANGE!

Did Azul know her? What was going on? Who was this beautiful lady? And, if I found the witch's magic wand, could I get it to make a cheese Danish?

I was still thinking about that wand when the new lady spoke.

"You look so FAMILIAR . . . and so does this place," she said, looking around thoughtfully.

"It should," Azul smiled. "I am Azul, your lost

husband. And this is your son, Blue Rider. You lived here long ago. Do you remember?"

Suddenly, the lady's whole face **Lit UP**, and tears streamed down her cheeks. "How could I forget?" she asked.

Then, in a SOFT voice, Azul told his story. . .

Years ago, Azul had fallen in love with a beautiful fairy named **DELIA**. Delia was smart and kind and good. Before long, the two got married and built a home in Sapphire City.

Delia was the guardian of the **Royal Ruby**, so when she married Azul and moved to Sapphire City, she brought the treasured **Ruby** with her. Of course, Azul was the guardian of the **Royal Sapphire**, which had been passed down to him as a child. Together, the couple made a perfect pair. Once the two gemstones were united, **Peace** reigned over the entire **KINGDOM OF FANTASY**. It was a wonderful time in cloudy

Sapphire City. Azul and Delia were magnificent leaders, and everyone was happy.

After a year, Delia and Azul had a baby boy they named Blue Rider. He had clear **BLUE** eyes and black hair — and a strange BIRTHMARK on his forehead. (You know, the blue heart that tied him to Tenderheart.)

One **HORRIBLE** day, the terrible witch Cackle sent one of her henchmen, Slivertooth the serpent, to kidnap the baby. Once she had the baby in her evil clutches, Cackle planned to ask for the two **gemstones** as ransom. So Slivertooth went to the nursery and hid under the baby's crib. But when Delia saw the **serpent**, she grabbed

Mother!

My son!

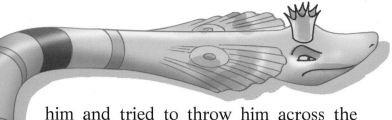

him and tried to throw him across the room. Unfortunately, the serpent was a lot faster than the fairy. He opened his mouth and bit her, **INJECTING** her with his wicked venom. The venom transformed her into a mean, *HORRIBLE* witch! The witch became known as Scorcher. She took the Royal Ruby back to her castle, which had also been transformed — it had become **TERROR CASTLE**.

Just as Azul had finished his story, the astronomer announced, "It's five o'clock. The **MORNING STAR** has risen. . . ."

We all raised our heads toward the sky, and through the open window in the ceiling, saw a bright spot **SHINING** in the sky.

A ray of light beamed down onto the lens that was placed in the center of the hall, which **divided** it into two rays. The RAYS hit the Royal Ruby and the Royal Sapphire simultaneously.

The two gemstones began to quiver, emitting an intense blinding light. Youch! Someone really should have handed out sunglasses! Anyway, when we were able to open our eyes again, we saw a remarkable sight. The two gemstones had become one, **PURE** and TRANSPARENT.

Another ray of sun hit the gem, which divided it into the seven colors of the rainbow. "Ooooh! Ahhh!" everyone exclaimed.

At last, the Ancient Gemstone Prophecy had been fulfilled!

I WANT TO
GO HOME!

Tenderheart turned to me and said *sweetly*, "Thank you, Music Mouse! Because of you, I found the true LOVE of my life!"

Delia added, "And I found my husband and son! And, thank *goodness*, I don't have to be a witch anymore. Being evil is so EXHAUSTING."

Azul said with a mysterious smile, "Actually, I

Music Mouse

think it's time we tell them your *true* identity, don't you, Music Mouse?"

Then he waved his hand, and instead of my gray tunic and **green** cape, I found myself dressed in my **KNIGHT'S ARMOR**, which I wore in my previous adventures in the Kingdom of Fantasy.

"Music Mouse is really **Sir Geronimo of Stilton**, the brave and famouse knight. He is the one who has saved the Kingdom of Fantasy many times before!" the king said.

Sir Geronimo of Stilton

Blue Rider couldn't hide his surprise.

"Then you're also a **knight**, mouse? I mean, Sir Geronimo? But, well, you didn't seem too **comfortable** on my horse," he commented.

I laughed. "I'm not the horse-riding kind of knight. I come from a faraway place called **Mouse Island**," I explained.

Azul put his arm around me. "And now you'll have yet another name. I hereby dub you Knight of the Treasured Gemstones!"

I suddenly found myself dressed in a simple white tunic and blue coat. I have to admit, I felt

Thank you for this honor!

Knight of the
Treasured Gemstones

a little silly in my new outfit. I mean, the tunic sort of reminded me of a lady's nightgown, and the coat kind of looked like a bathrobe. All I needed were some fuzzy slippers, and I'd be ready for bed!

Still, the last thing I wanted to do was to insult the king. Plus, as my dear aunt Sweetfur always told me, "It's not the clothes that make the mouse, it's the mouse that makes the clothes!" So I kept my thoughts to myself, bowed LOW to Azul, and squeaked, "Thank you for this honor. I will try to be worthy of it!"

Then everyone murmured to one another, "What a mysterious mouse! He has so many names and so many faces. . . ."

Who would've thought that I, Geronimo Stilton, would become such a MOUSE OF MYSTERY?!

Azul thanked me again for bringing PEACE

to the Kingdom of Fantasy. Then he said, "And now it's your turn, Sir Geronimo of Stilton, Knight of the Treasured Gemstones. What do you **WISH** for?"

I looked around, and thought, *I would like to live here forever, in this* MAGICAL *world where no problems exist and everything is peaceful.*

Azul smiled as if he had read my thoughts.

"You can stay as **long** as you want, Geronimo. . . ." he whispered in my ear. "But I believe that there are many who will **miss** you."

He was right. I began to feel terribly **homesick**.

"Well, I really like it here . . . and it's really great being the Knight of Gemstones, but . . . I actually think I'd like to go **home**!" I squeaked.

Then everyone hugged me and said, "We'll miss you, **knight**! Thanks for saving Sapphire City!"

Azul gave me a **blue** gemstone cup saying, "This is the *cup* of love."

I stared at the blue liquid swirling in the cup.

"All you have to do is drink this **potion** and think of all of those you love back at home, and your wish to go there will come true," the king said.

So I did. It wasn't hard to do.

And as I drank I thought: *I WANT TO GO BACK HOME I WANT TO GO BACK HOME I WANT TO GO BACK HOME I WANT TO GO BACK HOME I WANT TO GO BACK HOME I WANT TO GO BACK HOME I WANT TO GO BACK HOME*

YOU'RE ALIVE!

Suddenly, I was overwhelmed by a **swirling** whirlpool of cold water. Rats! Was this how I got home? By drowning in *freezing* water?

But just then I heard a familiar voice, "Look! He's alive! He opened his eyes!"

I opened my eyes wide and saw before me a familiar face. It was my nephew Benjamin! He hugged me and yelled,

"Uncle Geronimo, you're alive!"

I opened my mouth to say, "Of course, I'm alive," but found it was full of water, **algae**, and SAND. I spit them out, coughed for a while, and finally was able to say, "Where . . . where am I?"

I looked around and realized I was on a

tropical beach with white sand and palm trees. The ocean's *waves* lapped gently on the shore. Thea, Trap, and Benjamin were all staring at me.

I **stood** up and stammered, "The GEMSTONES . . . the witch . . . Azul . . ."

Thea hugged me as Trap **chuckled** and said, "Well, he hasn't lost his crazy imagination!"

"You fell in the WATER, and we looked for you everywhere!" Benjamin said, hugging me again.

"The waves carried you here! It's incredible that you survived, Gerry Berry," Thea added, wiping away a tear.

Even Trap squeezed my PAW.

"Glad you made it, Cuz. I MISSED your ugly mug," he said with a smile.

Thea's phone RANG and she passed it to me.

"Grandson! How dare you SCARE me half to death! Good to hear you're alive!" my grandfather's voice boomed. Then he passed the phone to Aunt Sweetfur, who said tearfully, "Geronimo, come home soon!"

The cell phone rang again. All my friends and

colleagues at *The Rodent's Gazette* wanted to know about me. And the paper had received over one million **EMAILS** from every corner of Mouse Island!

I was in shock. "I can't believe so many rodents were worried about me," I mumbled.

Benjamin laughed. "Of course! Everybody **loves** you, Uncle G!" he squeaked.

At that moment I felt like the *luckiest* mouse in the whole world. Holey cheese, it's great to be loved!

Everyone helped me back on board *The Silver Squeaker*, and Thea **PLOTTED** the course of navigation and set sails for home. Then they wrapped me in a warm, **fuzzy** blanket and gave me a steaming cup of hot cheese. Yum!

While we were sailing, I thought about how great it felt to be with my family, and about my amazing dream about the KINGDOM OF FANTASY.

When we got back home to New Mouse City, the first thing I did was write down the incredible adventure I remembered.

I wrote PAGES and PAGES and PAGES. . . .

I hope you liked the story, because it's the one you're just about to finish! Yep, this very one!

I wrote it with lots of love, because I really do love all my fans!

As far as the Kingdom of Fantasy goes, I haven't yet figured out how to get there while awake . . . but that's another story — another marvemouse story. I give you my word, or I'm not *Geronimo Stilton*!

FANTASIAN ALPHABET

ABOUT THE AUTHOR

Born in New Mouse City, Mouse Island, **GERONIMO STILTON** is Rattus Emeritus of Mousomorphic Literature and of Neo-Ratonic Comparative Philosophy. For the past twenty years, he has been running *The Rodent's Gazette*, New Mouse City's most widely read daily newspaper.

Stilton was awarded the Ratitzer Prize for his scoops on *The Curse of the Cheese Pyramid* and *The Search for Sunken Treasure*. He has also received the Andersen 2000 Prize for Personality of the Year. One of his bestsellers won the 2002 eBook Award for world's best ratlings' electronic book. His works have been published all over the globe.

In his spare time, Mr. Stilton collects antique cheese rinds and plays golf. But what he most enjoys is telling stories to his nephew Benjamin.

Be sure to read all of our magical special edition adventures!

THE KINGDOM OF FANTASY

THE QUEST FOR PARADISE:
THE RETURN TO THE KINGDOM OF FANTASY

THE AMAZING VOYAGE:
THE THIRD ADVENTURE IN THE KINGDOM OF FANTASY

THE DRAGON PROPHECY:
THE FOURTH ADVENTURE IN THE KINGDOM OF FANTASY

THE VOLCANO OF FIRE:
THE FIFTH ADVENTURE IN THE KINGDOM OF FANTASY

THE SEARCH FOR TREASURE:
THE SIXTH ADVENTURE IN THE KINGDOM OF FANTASY

THEA STILTON: THE JOURNEY TO ATLANTIS

THEA STILTON: THE SECRET OF THE FAIRIES

THEA STILTON: THE SECRET OF THE SNOW

Be sure to read all my fabumouse adventures!

#1 Lost Treasure of the Emerald Eye

#2 The Curse of the Cheese Pyramid

#3 Cat and Mouse in a Haunted House

#4 I'm Too Fond of My Fur!

#5 Four Mice Deep in the Jungle

#6 Paws Off, Cheddarface!

#7 Red Pizzas for a Blue Count

#8 Attack of the Bandit Cats

#9 A Fabumouse Vacation for Geronimo

#10 All Because of a Cup of Coffee

#11 It's Halloween, You 'Fraidy Mouse!

#12 Merry Christmas, Geronimo!

#13 The Phantom of the Subway

#14 The Temple of the Ruby of Fire

#15 The Mona Mousa Code

#16 A Cheese-Colored Camper

#17 Watch Your Whiskers, Stilton!

#18 Shipwreck on the Pirate Islands

#19 My Name Is Stilton, Geronimo Stilton

#20 Surf's Up, Geronimo!

#21 The Wild, Wild West

#22 The Secret of Cacklefur Castle

A Christmas Tale

#23 Valentine's Day Disaster

#24 Field Trip to Niagara Falls

#25 The Search for Sunken Treasure

#26 The Mummy with No Name

#27 The Christmas Toy Factory

#28 Wedding Crasher

#29 Down and Out Down Under

#30 The Mouse Island Marathon

#31 The Mysterious Cheese Thief

Christmas Catastrophe

#32 Valley of the Giant Skeletons

#33 Geronimo and the Gold Medal Mystery

#34 Geronimo Stilton, Secret Agent

#35 A Very Merry Christmas

#36 Geronimo's Valentine

#37 The Race Across America

#38 A Fabumouse School Adventure

#39 Singing Sensation

#40 The Karate Mouse

#41 Mighty Mount Kilimanjaro

#42 The Peculiar Pumpkin Thief

#43 I'm Not a Supermouse!

#44 The Giant
Diamond Robbery

#45 Save the White
Whale!

#46 The Haunted
Castle

#47 Run for the Hills,
Geronimo!

#48 The Mystery in
Venice

#49 The Way of
the Samurai

#50 This Hotel Is
Haunted!

#51 The Enormouse
Pearl Heist

#52 Mouse in Space!

#53 Rumble in
the Jungle

#54 Get into Gear,
Stilton!

#55 The Golden
Statue Plot

#56 Flight of the
Red Bandit

The Hunt for the
Golden Book

#57 The Stinky
Cheese Vacation

#58 The Super
Chef Contest

Don't miss my journey through time!